With my knees trembling again so badly that I could hardly stand, I stopped and, leaving the motor running, got out and took the paper. It was folded, and I didn't look at it until I was back in the truck with the door locked.

I unfolded it. On the paper, in pencil, a message was scribbled: IF YOU KNOW WHAT'S GOOD FOR YOU, STAY AWAY FROM THE RIVER AND MIND YOUR OWN BUSINESS.

I dropped that scrap of paper as though it had been hot, and my hands shook so badly I was afraid to drive. But I had no choice . . . .

MURDER
AND
OTHER
MISADVENTURES

Nadine Roberts

FAWCETT JUNIPER • NEW YORK

For Eddie and Darrell Roberts,
with love

Chapter One

IT WAS STILL hard for me to believe, but there we were, Daren and I, in Dad's old pickup truck. It was before daylight, during summer vacation, and we were on our way to the river. It was a shame that we couldn't be real friends. The summer had become quite a drag for me. If we hadn't hated one another for so long, it would have been fun to have someone to go to the river with every day.

We rode in silence for a while, then Daren said, "Does the radio work?"

I nodded. "Turn it on if you want," I said. We definitely needed something to break the silence, which I felt sure was as uncomfortable for Daren as for me.

He fiddled with the tuning dial, but every station seemed to be broadcasting the news. His switching stations was beginning to get on my nerves, and I finally said, "Leave it on the Gainesville station. After the news, there's a good music program."

He set the dial without comment, then settled into the corner of the seat, staring ahead. The national news finally came to an end, then we heard the familiar voice of a local announcer whom we'd both known all our lives.

"On the local scene," the announcer said in an impersonal voice, "Highway Patrol Sergeant Leonard reports that he definitely suspects foul play in the disappearance of a local resident.''

I glanced at Daren, and his expression said that he was as curious and attentive as I was.

''Miss Anne Morgan of 632 Tremont Street, affectionately known in and around Gainesville as Miss Annie, has been missing from her home for at least three days, and neither the police nor concerned neighbors have been able to determine her whereabouts. On Thursday morning Sheriff Daniel Hooper, who resides next door to Miss Annie, noticed a broken lock on her door. Upon entering the residence a bit later, he found traces of blood and some evidence of the house having been searched, suggesting that someone might have made a forced entry into the Morgan home.

''Miss Morgan, seventy-three years of age, has earned national recognition during the past few years with her unique sketches and oil paintings. Anyone having any information about Miss Morgan should call the Gainesville Police Department, the Chester County Sheriff's Office, or the state police immediately.''

''That's peculiar,'' I murmured, thinking about the woman everyone called ''Miss Annie.'' Although I had a fluttery, uncomfortable feeling in my stomach, the news report didn't seem quite real to me. It was as if they'd made it up, like fiction. I wasn't deeply upset because it simply didn't seem true. Maybe that was partly because I couldn't recall ever actually hearing anyone referring to Miss Annie ''affectionately,'' as the radio announcer had said.

In my experience, Miss Annie had always been an angry-looking old lady who wasn't especially friendly and who had never once expressed satisfaction with the way I had mowed her grass. It wasn't what she'd *said* about it, for she had rarely talked to me. Most of the time she would come to the door after I'd knocked about ten times, glare at me, frown at the freshly cut grass, hand me a five-dollar bill, and shut the door in my face. Grouchy or not, though, I hoped the police were mistaken and nothing bad had happened to her.

Suddenly I realized Daren had spoken, and I said, "Sorry, I didn't hear you."

"I only said that I wonder what's happened to Miss Annie," he said. "Somebody could have . . . well, robbed her, you know. Maybe killed her. I mean, all those rumors . . ."

"You mean about her having bushels of money hidden away somewhere?" I asked derisively. "You should know better than that! She's always been kind of a hermit, just exactly the kind of person people love to make up mystery stories about."

I glanced at Daren, and he didn't look pleased. Evidently I had irritated him with my automatic sarcastic response.

"I didn't say *I* believed the stories," he said, his voice tight and edgy. "I only said someone else might have believed them enough to . . . try to rob her or do something even worse."

"Okay, yeah, I see what you mean," I said, trying to smooth over my own impulsive error. "I hope nothing's really wrong. The idea of someone in Gainesville being robbed . . . murdered . . . just the *thought* of such things seems impossible. It gives me chills."

It was Daren's turn. "Gainesville's just a place, a town with ordinary people just like any other town," he said. "Crimes can happen here just as well as anywhere. We aren't immune. You should know better than *that*."

I gritted my teeth and didn't respond. Hadn't I known from the start that we wouldn't get along?

But circumstances have a way of creeping up on a person, and things that seem as if they'll last forever sometimes change. What I *didn't* know that morning was that soon Daren and I would have more than old grudges to occupy our thoughts, and that Miss Annie would become an awfully important part of our lives.

It would be a miracle if we made it through the day without fighting, and we had to tolerate one another for *two weeks*. Every day for fifteen days I would be the unwilling companion of Daren Levi Peterson. The fact that he found the prospect as repulsive as I did wasn't a bit of help. We had been enemies for eleven years, since the first time he'd made fun of my kinky hair back in kindergarten, which had inspired me to invent the nickname he'd hated ever since: "Jeans," because of his middle name.

In addition to my frizzy brown hair, I'd had zillions of freckles back then, and I was sure that every single one of them had been honored by some fine joke at one time or another. I remembered some of those dumb jokes as clearly as if I'd heard them only yesterday.

"What're we gonna play today?" Joey Aldrich had asked at recess back in second grade.

"I've got a great idea," Daren had replied, eyeing me with a malicious grin. "Get your ink pens, guys. We'll play dot-to-dot on Holly's . . . I mean Frizz-Head's freckles."

"You probably can't *see* my freckles well enough, Four-Eyes," I'd yelled back, and Daren cringed. He'd started wearing glasses only the week before.

That was the year my baby teeth fell out. I *always* lagged behind my classmates. They had all lost their front teeth in first grade. Daren had paid tribute to that momentous occasion by presenting me with a clumsily wrapped gift, again in front of the other kids during recess. I'd been gullible then, unwrapping the gift eagerly. It was a crisp, orange carrot.

4

So it had gone. We exhausted all the "fat" jokes when Daren had a chubby year or two. The "clumsy" jokes were at my expense during third and fourth grades, and we had shared the "ugly" jokes more or less equally.

"You are so ugly," I told him, "that when you were born, the doctor slapped your face, thinking it was your bottom."

"And you're *still* so ugly, you'd have to be twins to get any uglier," he replied. When we couldn't come up with anything new or original, we could always resort to "Frizz-Head" and "Jeans."

Oh, it was foolish and it was infantile; both of us knew that. But the pattern had been established so long ago that we would never be able to trust one another. At sixteen, juniors at Gainesville R-II High School in a few weeks, we'd pretty much given up the dumb insults, but we were still wary of one another. We would always be that; it was inevitable.

I had been wary enough the day before, the first time I'd seen Daren since the start of summer vacation. It was the fifteenth of August, hot and sultry, and I had gone to the river to cool off. The Spring River Cove access was only half a mile from our house, and it was pretty dangerous, always cold and always swift. I didn't actually go swimming there alone, but there was a little sandy cove where the water remained still and not too deep, and my parents didn't mind if I went there. They knew they could trust me. Like most of the Gainesville kids, I was a good swimmer, but hardly anybody actually swam in the treacherous current alone. We had all learned to be sensible about that.

I had a big beach towel, and I'd wade into the icy water and get myself cool, then come out and lie on the towel and read until I got too warm again. It was a pleasant way to spend a few afternoon hours, even if I was by myself. My buddies, Jeannie Smith and Rhonda Hobbes, were both off visiting relatives somewhere. They wouldn't be back until the Lions Club Festival in Riverton, a town nine miles west of Gainesville.

The Lions Club Festival was still two weeks away. It was an annual event that *nobody* missed; a really big bash, with a beauty pageant and canoe race and barbecue, and all kinds of games and competition and carnival rides.

Until then, I didn't have much to do. Mom and Dad both worked every day, and after I cleaned up the house, which took about an hour every morning, I was on my own. Without Jeannie and Rhonda to run around with, things were getting a bit boring.

So there I was at the Spring River Cove, alone until I heard a car coming. I looked up quickly, ready to split in a hurry if it wasn't someone I knew. It was, though. The first face I recognized was Daren's. He was with half a dozen other guys, all but two of them from Gainesville High School. They wouldn't bother me, though. The cove was too tame for a bunch of guys. Fifty yards or so up the bank, a big tree leaned out over a deep pool, and a rope swing hung from one of the limbs. Most of the kids loved swinging out over the water and diving in, or just turning loose and dropping into the pool. It was great fun, and I was right; the boys all headed for the rope swing. A couple of them waved to me, and I waved back, then went back to reading my book.

Pretty soon they were having so much fun, though, laughing and yelling and splashing around, that I couldn't concentrate on my reading. I put the book aside and propped myself on my elbows and watched them.

The funny thing was, Daren kept glancing toward me. I didn't care, but I did wonder what was on his mind. Maybe he had come up with a new joke, I thought, and was wondering whether to try it on me. Just in case, I tried to get my own brain in gear, but I couldn't think of a single good cutting insult that wasn't already worn out.

Then, wouldn't you know it, Daren left the other guys to the swing and started toward me. He wasn't chubby anymore, and the glasses were a thing of the past, too. In fact, if he'd been someone besides Daren Levi Peterson, he wouldn't look too bad at all, with those muscular legs and that thick, sandy hair.

But such thoughts were practically traitorous when they concerned Daren, and I surreptitiously patted my hair down and formulated an absolutely *nothing* expression, and waited. I would be cool and adult, whatever his intentions were. It was the only option I had, considering that I'd been unable to think of anything suitably offensive.

He stopped a few feet away, and finally he said, "Hi."

Well, that wasn't exactly earth-shaking. I said, "Hi." Neither of us smiled, or frowned, or anything.

"Okay if we talk a minute?" he asked. I nodded, and he sat down cross-legged and looked at the river. He sure was bland, maybe even just a touch ill at ease; it was hard to tell.

"What's on your mind?" I finally asked him.

He started drawing lines in the sand with his finger, still not really looking at me. Then he surprised me. "Do you still have that fiberglass canoe?" he asked.

"Sure," I said. "It's getting old and it looks pretty shabby, but it still handles better than any other canoe I've tried."

He nodded his agreement. "Have you entered the race yet?"

I shook my head. "I'm not entering this year," I said.

7

"Why not?"

"Because I'm not good enough to beat Tracey Sampson in the women's singles, and I'm too old for the girls' singles now. You know that."

We were talking about the canoe race that was probably the biggest event at the Lions Club Festival, or at least it was equal in importance to the beauty pageant, which I darn sure was *not* interested in entering. All the competitions were open to anyone who wanted to participate, and every year a few people came from towns as far as a hundred miles away. Lots of the hill-country logging people came to town for the festival, too, with the women looking a little shabby and work-worn, and the lumbermen always wearing beards, sweat-stained caps, jeans, and heavy work boots. Everybody was welcome, because it was a fund-raising day, and the entry fees alone made big money for the Lions Club. Aside from the fun, people liked the whole thing because it supported some real good causes, like buying glasses for people who couldn't afford them, or paying for cornea transplants and things of that sort.

But although there were always people from other towns, the majority of the competitors were either from Riverton or Gainesville, and the rivalry between the two towns was legendary, and it was intense. It wasn't just the festival, either. Whatever the competition—pigs at the county fair, high school football, golf tournaments at the Spring River Country Club, or Peewee softball—the competitors were always out for blood. Nobody seemed to know how such heated rivalry had gotten started, and nobody cared. On the surface, the two towns, similar in size and in the same county, were friendly. But beneath the friendliness, there was always competition. Like

8

our parents had apparently done, we grew up with it and carried it on and reveled in it.

Which was all beside the point for me this year, because I wouldn't be entering any of the competitive events.

Looking as if he might choke on his own words, Daren looked me right in the eyes, finally, and said, "Have you considered entering the mixed-doubles category?"

I snorted. "With whom?" I asked. "Everybody who's entering the doubles has had the same partner for years. There's nobody available that I know of, nobody who's any good, that is."

"Except me," Daren muttered.

I wasn't sure I'd understood him properly, so I asked him to repeat.

"I said, you and I could enter as partners," he said. He looked like he'd just bitten into a sour pickle.

I flopped over and sat up, and when I finally got my lower jaw back in place, I glared at him and said, "*Sure* you and I could enter as partners. When elephants fly!"

He winced and started to get to his feet; then, with a heavy sigh, he sat back down. Neither of us spoke for a couple of minutes.

Then he glanced at me, then away. "Look," he said, "let's be sensible for a few minutes. Call it a five-minute truce. Okay?"

"Yeah, I guess so," I mumbled. I was beginning to get a glimmer of what he was getting at.

"Whether you and I get along or not," he said, "the truth is that I'm the best male canoeist and you're the best female canoeist in our age group. Oh, I know Tracey Sampson's stronger than you, but she's a . . . an amazon, and besides, she must be at least twenty years old, and she never enters the doubles

9

anyway. So if we *could* work together, we'd have a decent chance.''

I nodded. I couldn't help it; he was right. But . . . Jeans and Frizz-Head, *partners*? Not a chance.

''Still, if we could have a shot at beating Riverton . . .'' I was talking to myself, actually.

''That's what I've been thinking,'' Daren said, a bit more enthusiastically. The sour pickle look had faded. ''If we could put everything else out of our minds, just concentrate on learning to work together—''

''We'd have to train every single day,'' I said. ''Have you considered that?''

''Yeah,'' he muttered. ''Every day starting tomorrow. Fifteen days, counting the race itself. That's a lot of time for us to spend together. Still . . .''

I took a deep breath and exhaled slowly, thinking it over. Finally I gritted my teeth and forced something roughly approximating a smile. ''I can do it if you can,'' I said.

He nodded. ''Me, too,'' he said. ''It'll be worth it if we can take the trophy from Riverton.''

''Okay,'' I said, ''if we take the trophy, which one of us gets to keep it till next year?''

Frowning, he thought it over. Then he said, ''I'll keep it the first month, then you get it for the next month, and so on. All right with you?''

''No way,'' I said. ''Alternating months is all right, but we'll draw straws for who gets it first. Short straw wins.''

He agreed. Then he said, ''And we'll share the entry fee. Fair enough? Ten bucks each?''

''Hey, we're using my canoe,'' I said. ''*You* shell out for the entry fee.''

''Now, wait, that's not . . .'' Then he stopped and nodded. ''I guess that's fair,'' he said, ''but who pays for repairs if we knock a hole in your canoe?''

I decided to be magnanimous. After all, I had enough patching stuff to practically build a whole canoe, in Dad's garage. "I'll take care of that," I said. "You supply your paddle, though. I only have one now. When should we start?"

"Whenever you say," Daren said, "only I need to be home by noon every day. I work at the lumberyard afternoons. Can we start *real* early?"

"Okay, I can do the housework after we get back," I said, "so I can be ready by five-thirty, unless that's too early for you."

"Five-thirty's fine," he said. "What'll we do about transportation? There must be half a dozen roads in to the river, but we need to practice on the actual racecourse. Only, that means hauling the canoe all the way up to Beaver Lodge Landing every morning, and taking it out at Willow Bend."

"I think Dad'll let me use the pickup," I said. "If you can get us home from Willow Bend, I'll get us to Beaver Lodge Landing every morning."

"Yeah, I can manage that," he said, with the first smile I'd seen. "I've saved a few bucks. Bought myself an old car. And my uncle has a rack I can borrow, to haul the canoe on."

So we got it all worked out. Mom and Dad had agreed, on condition that I would *never* go without my life vest unless I was actually standing on the bank. We'd had supper, and it was almost dark. I would have to go inside soon and get to bed. Canoeing every day would be exhausting, and I would need plenty of rest.

Enduring Daren's company every day for fifteen days without fighting would be the *real* strain, though. I wondered whether it would be worth the effort. It sure

11

wouldn't be easy, but it would be fantastic if we could beat Riverton.

Well, I would give it my best. Between Daren and me, things couldn't be any worse; that was one way to look at it.

It wasn't a heck of a lot of consolation.

Chapter Two

I STILL HAD misgivings just before daylight on Saturday morning, but it looked as if it would be a perfect day, weather-wise, and I couldn't keep from being excited about getting out on the water in the canoe.

I'd only been canoeing once all summer long. My dad had taken a day off from his roofing business back in June, just to spend the day with me. He enjoyed the river, too, and we had spent the whole day canoeing, fishing, and picnicking. It had been great fun, and I smiled, remembering.

My folks were terrific and I loved them fiercely. Mom worked for a company that produced medical supplies, to save college money for me, but she liked her job and never once caused me to feel guilty that I was the cause of her working so hard. I simply never had reason to complain about my parents, and I knew how lucky that made me.

They weren't exactly thrilled about the practice for the canoe race, but they understood the competitive spirit, and they also liked and trusted Daren, for some reason. They knew that both of us would be cautious and sensible on the river, but they were concerned with whether or not we'd be able to get along for two weeks. Since I had complained about Daren for years, they were well aware of how I felt about him.

The canoe wasn't very heavy, and I had no trouble putting it in back of our pickup truck. While it wasn't in use, I kept it upside-down on a couple of blocks. It was a simple matter to stoop and get beneath it, then straighten my back, holding one end over my head, walk it to the truck and rest it on the tailgate, then lift the other end and slide it forward until it touched the front end of the truck bed. I tied it down with a piece of ski rope then, and I was ready to go. Daren had offered to come by and help me load the canoe, but I had declined. He would meet me at Willow Bend.

I'd had my driver's license for several months, but I still didn't feel comfortable driving the truck, especially since it was still somewhat dark out. There wasn't anything difficult about it exactly, but it felt awkward. The practice I would be getting during the two weeks to come would make me competent, I decided as I drove carefully along the twisting gravel road leading to Willow Bend, which was little more than a gently sloping bank that was good for loading or unloading a boat. It would have been pretty in another season, I knew, but August had done her work well. At full sunrise the weeds by the roadside would appear dry and dust-covered, and few leaves would be stirring in the trees covering the slopes.

At last I made it to the flat strip along the river and turned in to the narrow approach to Willow Bend, where I saw Daren. He stood leaning against a faded blue car, and when he saw me, he checked to see that the car door was locked, then took a bright orange paddle and a life vest off the hood of the car and hurried to get into the truck with me. We would have a twelve-mile drive back through town and upriver to Beaver Lodge Landing. We didn't have any time to waste.

"Morning," he said, and I said, "Hi. Ready to go?"

14

He nodded, and I turned the truck around and started back the way I had just come.

"This is kind of complicated," he said after a while. "Too bad there isn't a simpler way."

"I know," I agreed, "but it'll only be for fifteen days."

"Fourteen after today," he said. I noted the hopeful tone in his voice. Already Daren was looking forward to the end of our enforced companionship!

Well, so was I. Spending two weeks in Daren's company wasn't my idea of a real good time either, but I would try to make the best of it.

That was when we heard the news broadcast about Miss Annie, which had led to the silly clash between us about crime in Gainesville, then silence.

By that time we had passed through town and were almost to the Beaver Lodge turnoff. The sky was lightening more every minute; we had to hurry, so Daren wouldn't be late getting back for work.

A long, graveled beach stretched beside the river at Beaver Lodge Landing, and there were two nice concrete boat ramps, a water faucet, picnic tables, and such. The place was deserted because of the early hour, but it was a popular put-in point for boaters. It would be full by the time Daren and I got back to get Dad's truck, so after we put the canoe on the ground, I parked where I wouldn't get blocked in, and got my paddle, life vest, and binoculars. There were still quite a few eagles nesting along the river. I loved watching them in the binoculars.

By the time I got back to the river's edge, Daren had the canoe in the water and was seated in the back. That position meant that he would have more control, and for a moment I almost objected just on principle. But he was stronger, and it made sense. I zipped the life

15

vest on, hung the binoculars around my neck, stepped into the canoe, and took my seat.

We pushed off, and in just moments we were moving downstream. It wasn't really full daylight yet, and on the water, the air felt chilly and invigorating. The trees lining the banks glowed in a dozen different shades of mist-shrouded green. Everything was beautiful, and the quiet was almost spooky. No matter how many times I came to Spring River, I supposed I would always be newly amazed at the absence of sound. Aside from that, I heard occasional bird calls and the rippling where the current washed through the leaves and limbs of fallen trees.

Daren broke the lovely silence then. "Are you going to paddle, or daydream?" he grumbled.

I leaned forward and dipped my paddle, pulling back with as much smooth force as I could without tipping us. I meant to put him out of stride and irritate him for being so grouchy, but all he said was, "That's more like it. Now let's see if we can work *together*."

We did work together then for a while, and when Daren said, "You're leaning too far," I straightened and kept going. And when I called "Switch," he did so, and on we went. We had a long way to go, learning how to match each other's strengths and compensate for our weaknesses, but it was beginning to look as if there might be some hope for us.

We weren't working at our full strength, knowing we would burn out quickly on our first day, but after a while my arms began to ache and a burning sensation began at a spot high on my spine. I didn't want to be the one to call for a rest, but I was ready to do just that when Daren said, "Let's break for a while, okay? I'm getting tired."

"So am I," I said, relieved. I put the paddle across my knees, then stretched and relaxed my arms and

16

shoulders. Daren rested, too, and we floated gently along on waist-deep water so clear that we could see an occasional small fish darting upstream on either side of the canoe. We were off to the side, out of the deep and swift channel. It was a perfect place to rest.

"Where are we?" I asked Daren. "I don't recognize anything here."

"I think the Blue Hole should be right around this bend," he said. "This *looks* like the right bend, anyhow."

I nodded. It was odd the way so many curves and bluffs on the river could look so much alike. A person could forget the little landmarks easily, and floods during rainy seasons washed them away as well. Gravel bars at the river's edge grew smaller or larger as a result of heavy rains; trees fell into the river, and new channels were carved here and there, to make Spring River an ever-changing and challenging adventure.

But the Blue Hole Daren had mentioned never seemed to change. It was an oddity; a very deep, wide pool right off the bank that didn't appear to be at all affected by the swift currents of the river, or even disturbed very much by the floods. There were lots of different stories about the origin of the Blue Hole. One said it was forty feet deep there, and that a spring in the bottom of the hole caused the murky blue color of the water. Even though the Blue Hole was *in* the river, the color of the water there was a deeper blue than the rest. Other stories assigned the origin of the place to everything from earthquakes to witchcraft, but I preferred the first story, since it sounded more plausible.

Although some mist still hung suspended over the water in places, the sun was well up by then. It hadn't actually broken over the high, forested bluffs on the east side of the river yet, but all the postdawn shadows had fled to wherever shadows go. I lifted the binoculars and began focusing them toward the left bank, far downstream. When we went around the point of the bend, I would see whether Daren's estimate of our distance was correct.

We cleared the bend, and from behind me Daren said, "Looks like I guessed it right. Is that a car down there on the bank beside the Blue Hole?"

"Tell you in a minute," I said. "I must've forgotten how to focus these darn things!" All I could see was a blur that faded from blue to green.

"I can see it now anyway," Daren said. "It is a car. Maybe somebody's fishing in the Blue Hole. There are supposed to be some monster catfish down there."

"There's supposed to be a pot of gold at the end of the rainbow, too," I said.

Just then a series of numbers and letters swam before my eyes, and I was startled until I figured it out. I was looking at a license plate. I didn't exactly *see* the letters, but I was aware of something; the letters formed an acronym I'd seen somewhere before. Having the license plate as a point of reference, I was able to get the binoculars focused at last. "It's a brown and white station wagon, old model, pretty badly banged up," I said. "There's a big dent in the back. And somebody's getting something out now. It looks like a . . . like a box of some kind. I wonder what he's doing."

"It's none of our business anyway," Daren grumbled. "We're rested; let's go on."

"Daren, would you please keep still just for a *minute*," I asked. Then I said, "On second thought, paddle us over toward the bank, where we won't be so visible."

"What for?" he demanded irritably. "We aren't doing anything wrong. Who cares if we're visible or not?"

I was becoming very nervous for some reason, and Daren wasn't helping any, but I didn't argue, and we floated nearer and nearer to the Blue Hole. I continued watching the man. He was having trouble with the box, as if it was heavy.

I heard Daren mumbling something about how it wasn't very nice to spy on people with binoculars. The canoe rocked then, and I lost the man for a moment. When I had him back in my sights, I could barely tell what was happening. He was stooping or sitting down or something, then he raised up, lifting, and suddenly an oblong box slid off the bank and sank into the Blue Hole! The man looked up then, and stood as though frozen, as he watched me watching him. He was short, maybe a bit on the chubby side. He wore a cap, and a beard, so I couldn't see much of his face. He was dressed in short-sleeved dull green coveralls. He spun around and got into the driver's seat of the station wagon. In a moment the car was out of sight.

"Well, have you seen enough?" Daren asked.

"I suppose so," I replied, puzzled. "Daren, it's really weird. Somebody just dumped a big box into the Blue Hole!"

"Who was it? Could you tell?"

I shook my head. "I couldn't see that well. It was a man wearing green coveralls, though. I wonder what the box was."

"Probably a fish trap," Daren said. "What did it look like?"

"Well," I said, thinking, "it was long and narrow. Kind of like a . . . shaped like a coffin." Odd, but that was the picture that came to mind.

"A coffin!" Daren hooted. "Holly, you're crazy!"

"I didn't say it *was* a coffin," I said. "It *wasn't*. But it was some kind of box that was rectangular, like a coffin is. Could that have been a fish trap?"

"Sure," Daren replied. "Fish traps can be shaped

like that. They're illegal, by the way, but that doesn't bother some people.''

"Well then, shouldn't we tell someone?" I asked. "Like the game warden, maybe?"

I had turned to face him by then, and Daren considered me thoughtfully. "I don't think we should mention it," he said at last. "We can paddle right over the Blue Hole and have a look, since he's gone, but we don't want any poachers to think we're interested in what they're doing, at least not until after the Riverton Festival's over with. We don't need any trouble, that's for certain.''

He was probably right, I thought, turning to get settled to paddle again. Like he'd said, it wasn't any of our business.

But as we paddled over the Blue Hole a couple of minutes later, I felt an uncomfortable chill. We couldn't see anything in that inky blue water, but I knew there was an oddly shaped box down there somewhere, and I wasn't sure that I even *wanted* to know what was in it.

Chapter Three

OUR TIMING WAS terrible on the first day, and although we hadn't meant to try for speed yet, the fact that it took us five hours to paddle the sixteen meandering miles of the racecourse showed us how much we had to accomplish in just thirteen days; the fourteenth day was the race itself.

We barely got back to town in time for Daren to make it to work, and I hurried to do the housework. By the middle of that afternoon I was so sore and stiff, I could barely move. Although I'd been running practically every day all summer, that exercise didn't seem to have done much to prepare me for paddling a canoe, and I dreaded the next day.

Nevertheless, I couldn't consider not going. I would suffer all kinds of agonies before I'd give Daren the chance to call me a quitter, and besides, I wanted to beat Riverton as badly as he did. Neither of us was sure who our primary competition would be, though we knew a lot of Riverton kids. We weren't worried about the competition from our own hometown because we were confident that we could beat everyone in our age group whom we knew to be into canoeing. Daren played basketball and baseball for Gainesville High, and I played volleyball and competed with fair success in track, so we were both in good shape and accustomed to athletic competition.

In good shape, that is, except for those muscles used in canoeing! Dad teased me a little about my aching arms and shoulders, and Mom said, "Are you sure you want to skip church for practice in the morning? Maybe it would be better to rest tomorrow."

It was a tempting idea, but I shook my head. "We need every hour of training that we can manage," I said. "We didn't get our strokes synchronized very well yesterday, and we've got to get that worked out before we can concentrate seriously on speed. Besides, it'll only be bad for the first hour or so in the morning—I hope."

"What was the record for your category of mixed doubles last summer?" Dad asked.

"Almost exactly two hours, for the sixteen miles," I said.

Dad whistled, raising his heavy black brows. "That's pretty fast, isn't it? Eight miles an hour . . . Do you think you and Daren can beat that?"

I shrugged, and winced. "Can't tell yet," I said, "but I sure hope so. It would be terrible to go through all this for nothing."

Mom winked at me, smiling. "Look at it this way," she said. "Maybe you won't win, but you'll be in good shape for volleyball when school starts."

I helped Mom wash up the supper dishes, and went to bed. Since I'd been old enough to date, I'd gotten into the habit of going to bed early on Saturday evenings when I was home, mostly to give Mom and Dad a little privacy. Mom was thirty-six years old and Dad two years older, but they seemed so young, often acting as romantic as a couple of teenagers. My friends Rhonda and Jeannie were always teasing about how handsome my father was, and they were right. He was

22

tall and just hefty enough; his sparkling blue eyes and curly black hair were attractive, and his teasing, good-humored personality seemed to appeal to everyone.

Mom was as pretty as could be, too. She was three inches shorter than my five feet five, making her the petite one in our family. She, too, had blue eyes, but her hair, which she wore in a boyish cut that made her seem even tinier, was dark brown. I wished I had inherited her smoothly waved hair instead of my father's kinky curls, but Mom insisted that my hair, which Daren had long ago chosen to call "frizzy," was actually all right.

Anyway, when I left them, they were sitting on the sofa together, with the stereo playing some lazy-paced instrumental stuff that I didn't exactly hate to miss. Once in my room, I remembered that I'd intended to ask whether they had heard anything more about Miss Annie, but I decided to wait until the next day.

The alarm buzzing in my ear finally broke into my nonsensical dream, and I groaned as I sat up in bed. Was I ever sore! I stumbled to the bathroom and turned the shower on as hot as I could stand it, and by the time I came out, I was wide-awake and not quite so stiff any longer. After devouring a couple of scrambled eggs and a big glass of juice, I slipped outside and loaded the canoe. Every day we would be hauling it back to my house on the rack on Daren's car, then he would drive me back up to Beaver Lodge Landing to get Dad's truck. As Daren had said, it was complicated, but there wasn't any easy way to do it.

The early morning air felt unusually chilly, and I decided to take an old flannel shirt that was hanging in the garage. Daren shivered when he got into the truck with me at Willow Bend. He wore an unpleasant expression, and was clearly in a rotten mood.

"I was cold, waiting," he grumbled without even a greeting. "What took you so long?"

"Daren, I got here at the same time yesterday," I said. "But if you're already cold, we could stop by your house to get a jacket. I brought a long-sleeved shirt."

"We can't afford the time," he said. "I was almost late for work yesterday. We've got to make better time today."

I wanted to be pleasant, but his attitude wasn't making it easy. But everyone has a bad day now and then, I told myself. I'll just keep cool and he'll lighten up soon.

"It'll be warmer by the time we get there," I said, "but you can turn the heater on if you want to."

"That's ridiculous," he muttered. "Imagine using a heater in the middle of August!"

"If you're not warm enough, what does the date matter?" I asked reasonably.

He glowered, then reached to switch the radio on. I wondered whether he thought that would warm him, but I decided to just let him stew, since that seemed to be all he was going to do anyway.

The news broadcast had just started, and I listened with only scant attention to comments about the Middle East and Washington, D.C. I became more alert with the start of the local news, though.

"There is still no explanation of the apparent disappearance of Miss Anne Morgan, of this city," the announcer said. "However, it has been reported by Sheriff Hooper that an unidentified man with a heavy beard was seen lurking near the Morgan residence last Tuesday night, near midnight. Neighbors and friends of Miss Morgan are deeply concerned, and law enforcement officials continue to urge anyone with *any* information about Miss Morgan to come forward immediately."

A picture of the bearded man and the coffin-shaped

box sliding into the water of the Blue Hole flashed through my mind, and I shivered.

"You're cold, too," Daren said accusingly. "I'll turn the heater on."

I didn't respond, but I hadn't shivered from the cold. "I wish they'd find out what happened to Miss Annie," I said after a while. "It scares me, thinking of . . . things that might have happened."

"Yeah," Daren agreed morosely, and fell silent.

The news broadcast continued. "Another unsolved crime continues to trouble the Cedar Hills community. The person who took an undetermined amount of money at gunpoint from the teller at the drive-in window of the Cedar Hills State Bank is still at large. That robbery took place just after the bank opened on Wednesday of last week."

"Crimes everywhere," Daren muttered.

"It seems that way," I agreed. "It's funny; nothing much ever happens around here, and then all this at once. Cedar Hills is only thirty miles up in the hills."

"Twenty-six."

Well, so much for my efforts at conversation with Daren! Phooey on him, I thought. Who needed his grumpiness?

We rode the rest of the way in silence; we unloaded the canoe in silence, and when I had parked the truck and was ready to go, Daren only said, "Let's try to start out nice and smooth. No power strokes until we're really working together."

I said, "Okay," and we pushed off.

I knew it would be miserably hot in a little while, after the sun made it all the way to break over the tree-tops. For the time being, though, it was uncomfortably chilly, and I was glad I had brought the shirt along. For a while we would have to depend mostly on our paddling to warm us.

We had things going pretty nicely for half an hour or so. We tried—and generally succeeded—dipping our paddles at the same time and to the approximate same depth, and pulling back with as close as possible to equal force. After every ten strokes, we switched sides, and that tended to correct the errors resulting from any lack of synchronization. The point was to waste no motion, to see that every ounce of expended energy would propel us downstream, without any time- and energy-wasting slips to either side.

We made practically no sound at all, and that kind of silence tends to become hypnotic after a while. So when a huge gray crane whooshed up from the nearest bank, it startled me badly, and I leaned too far into the stroke, swinging us sideways. The canoe rocked, but didn't tip.

But it was too much for Daren's foul mood. Hurrying to get us straightened out, he yelled, "Were you born this dumb, Frizz-Head, or did you take private lessons!"

Whirling around toward him, forgetting in my fury that I was in a canoe, I yelled, "Listen, *stupid* . . ."

That was as far as I got, because I was toppling over backward. The shock of the icy water closing over me drove everything else from my mind, as I struggled to get my feet on the graveled river bottom and my head above water.

When I came up gasping, I could barely keep my footing in the swift, shoulder-deep current. Though it had seemed like ages, only seconds had passed, and I pushed myself up and forward, barely getting my hands on the overturned canoe just as Daren came up sputtering on the other side. The canoe floated upside down, and without a word to each other, we tipped it upright, bringing up one paddle with it. But the canoe was half-full of water, and we would have to get it to the bank to empty it. The other paddle, mine, floated merrily downstream.

Pushing the canoe was difficult at first, but it became easier as we waded into shallower water. However, it was even colder in that chilly breeze than it had been underwater, and my teeth chattered.

Daren's didn't. His jaws were too tightly clenched.

At the bank we leaned the canoe over, emptying it, then put it back in the water and got in. Neither of us had said a single word.

Daren paddled us out into the current again, and moved us downstream toward my paddle. I could barely see it in the distance, but soon we drew closer. I huddled in the front of the canoe, shivering. The water running off our clothes was already an inch or so deep in the bottom of the canoe.

When we came up beside my floating paddle, I was so cold, I could barely move to reach for it, but I managed, taking care not to tip us again. I began to paddle, awkwardly at first, but after a couple of minutes, I could feel the proper rhythm coming back. Not that it mattered; the canoe race could darn well do without me! I was finished! Once I got home, I would . . .

"Take that shirt off!"

"What?" I mumbled. What was he talking about?

"I said take that long-sleeved shirt off," Daren said in his ordinary bossy manner. "Your skin will get dry in a minute without the shirt. Then you won't be so cold."

It made sense, so I removed the life vest and unbuttoned the sopping shirt and peeled it off, dropping it into the bottom of the canoe.

Just then I felt the blessed, wonderful warmth of the first rays of sunshine. It felt so good! My teeth still chattered and I still shivered, but I was already feeling

27

better. I hated putting the wet life vest back on, but I had promised not to go without it, so I put it on.

For some unfathomable reason, my anger seemed to have evaporated, and as I replayed the whole ridiculous scene in my mind, I began to grin. I kept seeing Daren's face when he came sputtering out of the water, and soon my shoulders began to shake with laughter. I knew Daren would be furious, but I couldn't help it, and soon I was laughing so hard, I could not paddle, and I couldn't quit laughing either.

And in a moment I became aware that behind me, Daren was laughing, too!

"Listen, Holly," he said when we had finally recovered from the ridiculous laughter, "I'm sorry I was such a jerk. It was my fault, all of it. I was stiff and sore and cold, and like a spoiled brat, I took it out on you. But I won't be so hateful anymore, I promise."

"Okay," I said, starting to giggle again. "As long as you're, uh . . . cooled off now, we'll forget it."

"We'll never forget it unless we're good and dry before we get home," Daren said, "because if our parents find out what happened, they're never gonna *let* us forget it!"

Chapter Four

AFTER I GAVE some thought to Daren's observation, I told Mom and Dad about overturning the canoe anyway. I hated to do it, but I was fairly sure they wouldn't bar me from the river forever. Then for a little while after I told them, I wasn't quite so certain, because Mom, especially, was pretty upset. The accident scared her, of course. Though a lot of the river wasn't deep, some parts were. And she was also well aware that there was more to be concerned about than the depth. The treacherous current and the trees that had fallen into the water created most of the real danger.

They discussed it, and I tried to reassure them. We would *not* quarrel in the canoe anymore, I promised, and we did always wear our life vests.

Then at last Dad began to come around. "I'm beginning to think it's not so awful. In fact, I'm rather glad it happened," he told Mom, "and I'd have given a dollar and a quarter to've been there to see it." He was even beginning to smile by then.

"You're *glad* it happened?" Mom asked. "Glenn, they were two kids out there by themselves. Anything could have happened! They might have drowned!"

"I know, Patty," Dad replied, comforting her, "and I'm not making light of it. But now that it *has* happened, now that they've learned how easily a canoe can flip over, they'll be more careful. Holly and Daren have sense; they won't be so careless again. And they're both excellent swimmers."

"Well, all right," Mom said, obviously reluctant, "but sensible or not, it's scary. Too many scary things have been happening lately. It's making me nervous."

I figured Mom meant the things Daren and I had heard on the radio. "Has there been any more news about Miss Annie?" I asked them.

Dad shook his head. "Just a lot of speculation," he said. "Everyone seems to be talking about it, but I don't think the investigation has turned up anything useful. They haven't even been able to locate Miss Annie's sister yet. She's supposed to be living somewhere in Chicago, but they can't seem to find her."

I hadn't even known there was a sister. "Is she as old as Miss Annie?" I wondered.

"Maybe ten years or so younger," Mom said. "If the police could locate her—well, they're hoping Miss Annie simply went to visit her sister."

"But the lock on her house was broken," I said, "and her house was ransacked. And wasn't there some . . . some blood in the house?"

"The house wasn't exactly *ransacked*," Dad said. "I heard that some drawers were left standing open— just kind of messy, which wasn't like Miss Annie at all. And as for the blood, it wasn't much; just traces in the kitchen sink and on a paring knife that was on the drainboard. Supposedly they'll be able to tell— well, whether it was human blood, you know? And whether or not it was Miss Annie's blood type and all that."

"It's creepy," I said. "This all sounds like some scary movie."

"I'm afraid it's real enough," Dad said, "although

there's no proof of any actual crime having been committed yet. And to make everything even more difficult, the investigative force, if you can call it that in a little place like Gainesville, has lost a man."

I didn't know what he was talking about, and when he saw my puzzlement, Dad went on.

"Haven't you heard the latest bad news? Sheriff Hooper's son was skydiving yesterday. He lives on the East Coast; he's in college. Anyway, he was hurt. Hooper and his wife flew out there. The boy . . . something's wrong with his eyes. Otherwise he doesn't seem to be too badly injured."

"Are you saying the sheriff's son is blind?" I asked, shivering.

"Not blind, but his eyes were damaged. I believe they said it was detached retinas on both eyes. It can be repaired with surgery, or at least that's what I was told."

"And the Hoopers will have insurance, surely," Mom said.

Dad combed his fingers through his curly hair. "According to Jim Sampson, that kind of sport activity wasn't covered by the policy. In fact, it was specifically excluded. It's going to be a real financial burden, but the most important thing is that he'll be well eventually."

None of us knew very much about the sheriff or his family. They had moved to Gainesville only a year before, and our sheriff of many years died unexpectedly soon afterward. Mr. Hooper, who had been in law enforcement in his former town, had been appointed to complete the former sheriff's term. I suppose someone had known him well enough, or he wouldn't have been so readily accepted in Chester County. But all I knew was that they lived next door to Miss Annie. I had seen Mrs. Hooper in their yard a couple of times while I was mowing Miss Annie's grass. It was sad that their son had been injured. I'd never actually known him, but to have his eyes damaged—it seemed about the worst possible kind of injury to me.

While I brooded about that, Mom came up with a suggestion that didn't exactly thrill me. I felt restless and fidgety just thinking about it, and that spoiled the rest of Sunday afternoon.

"Your father and I drove past Miss Annie's house on the way home from church," Mom said, "and her grass needs cutting. You should do that after you get back from the river tomorrow."

I felt the goose bumps coming. "But she's . . . she's not at home," I protested. "I've never mowed her grass when she was gone."

"What difference does that make?" Dad asked.

"Well, I . . . I don't know," I mumbled. "It just seems odd or something. I mean, maybe she's . . . uh . . . not even *alive*."

"There's no evidence of any such thing! And you've cut Miss Annie's grass for two years," Mom reminded me. "You agreed to keep an eye on it and cut it whenever it was needed, right?"

I nodded.

"Then go and cut her grass tomorrow."

What could I say? Mom was right, of course. I had taken on the responsibility. It hadn't occurred to me to ask Miss Annie whether I should continue to mow her grass if she should happen to disappear someday. Leaving a broken front door lock. And her house all messed up. And blood in the kitchen sink . . . and on a knife. . .

On Monday morning when I went out to load the canoe, I discovered that I had left my binoculars lying outside all night, and they were wet with dew, which made me pretty aggravated at my own carelessness. I wiped them off and put them in the truck seat. So far, I hadn't seen any eagles at the river, but I felt sure that I would sooner or later. They were so magnificent; I didn't want to miss a chance to observe if one should appear.

When I got to Willow Bend, Daren hadn't arrived yet, and I waited alone for a few minutes. At first it was quiet and peaceful. Then I remembered that I would have to cut Miss Annie's grass that afternoon, and an eerie feeling came over me. I couldn't seem to relax any longer. I kept wanting to look over my shoulder, and I was glad when Daren came.

He was certainly in a better frame of mind than on the preceding day, yet not exactly full of good cheer either. He kept sneezing.

"Gee, you seem to have gotten a cold somehow," I teased as we were leaving. He gave me a half-hearted grin, and I had the most peculiar reaction: He was just so cute there for a second . . .

"Yeah," he grumbled, but good-naturedly, "it must be this early morning air that did it. And by the way, how come *you're* not red-eyed and sneezing? You got just as wet and cold as I did."

"Chicken soup, I suppose," I replied.

"You're joking! Your mother didn't actually feed you chicken soup?"

"Yep. She didn't exactly do it the absolutely right way," I told him. "She didn't start the project in the henhouse, since we don't have a henhouse. Actually, she opened a can and dumped it into a bowl, then she heated it in the microwave. But she made me eat chicken soup, just the same. That's what I got for going home and confessing what happened. How about you? Did you tell your folks about our dunking?"

Daren shook his head. "No way," he said. "There

never was quite the right moment for a confession. Besides, I figured it would be kinder *not* to tell them.''

"But *you* got a cold, and *I* got chicken soup," I said. "You really should consider total honesty sometime. It pays, as you can see with a glance at my glowing, *un*-feverish complexion."

"Speaking of your glowing, unfeverish complexion," Daren said with a sideways glance in my direction, "I've been meaning to ask you . . . whatever happened to your freckles, anyway?"

Not even for one second did I wonder whether this was the same old assault with intent to inflict emotional pain. I knew better. There was a difference—well, in tone, sort of. But that's not quite it. The difference was more than audible. It was practically in the air around us, and I was intensely aware of it. Yet somehow I was able to reply casually.

"My freckles? Gee, I don't know," I said. "I guess they went to the same place your glasses went, huh?"

What had made the difference between us? I really had no idea, but I felt almost comfortable with Daren right then. It was a strange but satisfying feeling to be at ease with him for the first time in my life. I smiled, at least on the inside, while I drove, and I could sense him looking at me every now and then. He had stopped sneezing, and when I glanced his way once, he seemed contented.

We unloaded and got under way. It wasn't nearly so cool as Sunday morning had been, though the mist hung even more heavily over the water. We intended to try for smoothness and speed both this time, and as soon as we were settled and comfortable with the feel of the current beneath us and the paddles in our hands, we went to work.

We went for a long time without talking or pausing, and I was falling under the spell of the rhythmical movement when I realized that Daren had stopped paddling. I lifted my paddle, too, and heard him whisper, "Over there—left bank."

I looked, but didn't see anything. "Keep looking," he whispered. "Something moved in the brush by that little road. Probably a deer."

After a moment I, too, saw limbs moving, but I couldn't tell what it was. Then suddenly I could. I could see, not the whole person, but the blue legs—jeans legs. Somebody was on the bank, hiding in the brush.

Daren had evidently seen it by then, too. "The binoculars," he whispered.

I lifted the binoculars and tried to focus, but I could see nothing but a blur. Frustrated, I tried again, before I realized what had happened. Moisture had accumulated on the lens because I'd left the binoculars outside overnight. They would have to dry on the inside before I'd be able to see anything. Irritated, I put them down.

"Did you see who it was?" Daren asked quietly.

"No," I grumbled. "I've let the lens get clouded. Did you see anything?"

He sounded troubled when he answered. "I didn't see who it was," he said, "but whoever it was, he was definitely watching us. He's gone now. Must've come down that field road to the river, but that's an awfully long way. I don't like it."

"But, Daren, it could have been anybody," I said. "Gosh, the river's not exactly private, you know."

"I know that," he said, "but unless he was, you know, *deliberately* watching us, why would he hide in the brush? I mean, it would've been a lot simpler for him if he'd stood there on the bank. It just gave me the creeps, you know? to feel like someone was . . . spying on us or something.''

We resumed our paddling then, but I couldn't get lost in the hypnotic thing like before. I kept glancing at both banks, and seeing things that weren't there. I wished he hadn't said those things about someone spying on us. Like he'd said, it gave me the creeps.

When we came to the Blue Hole, I couldn't take my eyes off the place. Was there something different? No, of course not. It was my imagination.

"What's the matter?" Daren asked. "You're out of stride."

"Just this place," I answered.

"What about it?"

"There's something in a big box down there," I reminded him. "I forget it usually, and then suddenly I'll think about it. I wonder what it was."

"I thought we agreed it was just a fish trap," Daren said.

"Well, maybe," I said, "but if it was a fish trap, wouldn't the person who put it there probably come back and check it early? We've never seen anyone here since Saturday morning."

"Doesn't mean he hasn't been here," Daren said. "He saw us watching him that day. Maybe he's coming earlier to check his trap. Don't get nervous for nothing, Holly. It was just a fish trap!"

We finished the course in reasonable time, in spite of the interruptions, and we both felt pretty good about the progress we'd been able to make in just the three days. It did seem like we might have a chance, but of course, it was too soon to tell.

Back home at last, I unloaded the canoe and backed the truck up to the little ramp Dad had made me for loading the lawn mower. I would go inside and have some lunch, clean up the house a bit, and then go on to Miss Annie's. I didn't want to do it, for some reason, and my hesitation made absolutely no sense. But it had to be done, so I drove the lawn mower into the back of the truck and slammed the tailgate shut. Like it or not, I'd go and mow that yard!

Chapter Five

I WASN'T EXACTLY speedy about doing the house-work, but I got it done at last. For a while I tried to convince myself that it would be all right for me to wait until Dad came home from work; he could go to Miss Annie's house with me. But I knew that was foolish, and unfair as well. Dad would be tired when he came home, and I had no right to impose upon him for something so pointless and silly.

The truck motor rumbled and grumbled. It didn't seem to be running very well, and I drove slowly at first. That was when I noticed an automobile pulling away from the curb about a block from my house. It followed me, though at my slow speed, it would have been easy and safe for the driver to have gone around. Then as I glanced into the rearview mirror again, I saw that it was an old station wagon—the same one I had seen at the Blue Hole on Saturday morning, I was almost certain! I couldn't see the driver at all because of the angle of the afternoon sunlight, and he wasn't following terribly close anyway.

Irritated but not especially disturbed, I kept glancing in the mirror. Because I hadn't gotten comfortable about driving the pickup yet, I never liked someone following me. It made me a little bit nervous, and aside from the flashes of memory from what I had seen at the Blue Hole, I wished he would go around.

He didn't, though. Then the truck motor smoothed out and started running properly, and I increased my speed a bit. When I came to the Tremont Street intersection, I felt relieved. Finally I would get off the main street, and the station wagon would go on.

The station wagon turned in to Tremont Street behind me.

Miss Annie's house, a couple of blocks down, was empty, of course. So was the house next door. According to Dad, the sheriff and his wife had gone to be with their son. On the opposite side of Miss Annie's house, a large vacant lot had grown up with weeds. There were a couple of houses across the street, but everything appeared deserted. There was no traffic except myself and the driver behind me.

I didn't want to stop, and at first I thought I would go on around the block and come back. Then at the last moment, knowing that my discomfort was certainly not very logical, I turned in to Miss Annie's driveway. With my attention on the turn, I couldn't watch the other driver as he passed behind me—but he gunned the motor and sped up the street, and by the time I could look, all I could see was the dust-covered and dented rear end of the automobile.

I backed the pickup into a low spot and unloaded the lawn mower, but all the while I wondered about the station wagon. Why had the driver followed me so slowly, then sped away after I stopped? On the other hand, another part of my mind reasoned, maybe he hadn't actually been following me. He'd only happened to be *behind* me. Maybe he had simply had some business on Tremont Street, as I'd had.

The grass did need cutting badly, and I started the lawn mower. But it was so noisy that it bothered me—

not the actual noise, but the fact that it drowned out all other noises. What else did I expect to hear? Nothing in particular, of course, but with only that one sound to hear, I felt defenseless. I couldn't seem to keep myself from frequent glances toward the street, and toward Miss Annie's windows as I circled her house. It seemed as though there must be eyes somewhere behind those windows that looked so black—eyes that could watch me, but that I could not see.

Since I wasn't strictly attentive to my work, I ran over a paper bag that had been concealed in the grass, and the shredded pieces scattered. Such an unattractive mess had always been intolerable to Miss Annie, so I shut the motor off and began gathering up the scraps of paper. Then, since the grass was rather high, I decided that I might as well make sure it didn't happen again. Quickly I walked back and forth across the uncut part of the yard, but I only found one other scrap. It was a rectangular piece of thin paper, with faded carbon printing on it, the carbon of some official form or other. I didn't recognize what it was, nor did I look very carefully, but I noticed the faded name of Anne Morgan, and some numbers. It was probably only trash, but perhaps not; it might be something she would need. I dropped it into the little toolbox Dad had attached to the frame of the lawn mower and closed the lid. When— or if—Miss Annie came home, I would ask whether the paper was something she needed to keep.

I finished mowing the grass then, and loaded the lawn mower back in the truck. Now that it was finished, I felt terribly pleased with myself for my fine, responsible behavior. Then I laughed at my own foolishness, remembering how I had tried to get out of mowing Miss Annie's yard. I had done it, though, and no ghost had lurked in the hedges after all. Nothing had happened.

Nothing, that is, except the station wagon that had . . . followed me?

Mom called soon after I got back to the house. She and Dad wanted to have dinner in town instead of coming straight home from work. Did I want to come and join them? I declined, since I still hadn't showered. I told her I would fix myself a sandwich instead.

I didn't really mind being alone, but after a little while, the house did seem awfully quiet, and I wished Jeannie or Rhonda were in town so I could have someone to talk with.

Then I thought of Daren, and of the station wagon. Before I knew what I was doing practically, I had dialed his number. He seemed surprised at my call, but not displeased.

"I saw that station wagon again," I told him.

"What station wagon?" he asked.

"The one we saw at the Blue Hole on Saturday," I said. "It followed me over to Miss Annie's today."

"Why?"

"*I* don't know why," I said. "I didn't talk to him—or whoever was driving. I don't know whether it was a man or a woman."

"What difference does it make?" Daren asked then.

"Well, it doesn't exactly make any difference," I said, "but don't you think it was sort of strange, that he followed me, I mean?"

"Sure, if that's what he was actually doing," Daren said, "but how do you know he was following you? I mean, just because he was behind you, that doesn't mean he was deliberately following."

"I know," I said, "but I think he was. Anyway, it made me feel pretty weird. I mean, I know we didn't actually *see* anything that day. We don't really know what he was doing, and I know it probably wasn't anything. It just . . . bothers me, that's all."

"Yeah, I guess it would, at that," Daren surprised me by agreeing, "especially after this morning."

I didn't even know what he meant for a moment, then I remembered the person in the bushes, watching us.

"It's a good thing I'd forgotten about that," I said, "or I never would have been able to stay and mow the whole yard. Do you suppose we ought to tell our folks about it?"

Daren laughed. "What would we say?" he asked. "Think about it, Holly. Nothing happened. That person on the bank this morning—it's just like the station wagon. We *think* he was watching us, but it doesn't really make any sense. Why would anyone go to all that trouble just to watch two kids paddle a canoe? It's just too silly. I've about decided the person in the bushes was just . . . you know . . . uh . . . using the bathroom or something."

"And the guy wasn't really following me today, even though he was parked practically at my house to start with, and the person at the Blue Hole wasn't doing anything that was any of our business, and he probably didn't know who we were anyway, and . . ." I ran down. I was a little irritated, but the most frustrating thing about it was there was no *sense* to that either.

He was right, though. What was there to tell Mom and Dad about? Nothing.

"Besides," Daren went on, "if we told our folks, it would look like we were scared or something, and that would make them scared. I mean, people are sort of nervous in Gainesville, with all the stuff happening . . . We're not used to it here. The point is that our folks might get uptight and want us to stop practicing, see? And if we're gonna beat Riverton, we've got to practice."

"I suppose you're right," I grumbled. "I guess I'm just getting worried for nothing. Miss Annie and the bank robbery and all—they don't have anything to do with us.''

"Listen, Holly,'' Daren said, ''tell your folks if you want to. I didn't mean to be saying I didn't want you to. It's just that . . . well, it seems to me that there isn't anything concrete to tell them, see?''

In the end, I agreed with Daren. If I did tell them about my vague fears, they might take it too seriously and make us stop going to the river. And I didn't have to feel guilty about not telling them either, since, as Daren had said, there really wasn't anything to tell!

Chapter Six

ON THE WAY to Willow Bend the next morning, I thought about how pleasant it was to be able to talk to Daren without fighting. Our getting along probably wouldn't last, I reflected, because we had been involved in our own personal cold war for so long that the animosity had become natural and expected. Everybody knew about it, of course, and for all those years, when things started getting dull at school, someone would try to stir us up just for the entertainment. It had never failed to work, either.

Nevertheless, it felt good not to dread seeing Daren. I didn't exactly want to relax my guard yet, but if one of us didn't revert to our habitual antagonistic behavior pretty soon, it was going to start looking like we might be in danger of becoming actual friends.

He was thoughtful when I picked him up, and didn't have much to say until, as had become our standard practice, we listened to the news broadcast. Again Miss Annie's disappearance was the subject of the local news, and we listened intently.

Earlier, when there had still been hope that she had gone to Chicago to visit her sister, those who were investigating the case had seemed to relax their fears of foul play to some extent. But those hopes were finished now, for the sister had been found, on a Mediterranean cruise! And she hadn't heard from Miss Annie in months. They had never been terribly close, the sister said, and she hadn't the slightest notion of what might have happened. The only thing the sister seemed to know was that Miss Annie had, in fact, habitually kept large amounts of cash in her home. The rumors were actually true! The women had argued about that at one time, with the sister failing in her attempt to convince Miss Annie to put her money in a bank.

The investigation would be intensified, and they were especially concerned about identifying the stranger whom a neighbor claimed to have seen lurking about the house before Miss Annie was known to be missing. That might prove to be a problem, I thought. Who would be likely to come forward and admit that he'd been hanging around the scene of a suspected crime?

Furthermore, the blood in Miss Annie's kitchen, they had learned, was almost certainly Miss Annie's blood!

At that commentary, my stomach gave an unexpected lurch, and I opened the window to the chilly morning air. "Sorry," I mumbled when I could talk. "I felt queasy there for a moment."

Daren said, "So did I. You know, I haven't thought too much about Miss Annie until now. I figured she had just gone off someplace, and they were worrying for nothing. I didn't actually know her; she was pretty peculiar, wasn't she?"

It gave me the shivers to hear Daren talk about Miss Annie in the past tense, but I didn't mention it. "I never talked to her very much," I told him. "She was mostly just grouchy to me. I figured she didn't like teenagers or something. But as for her being 'peculiar,' she's an artist, you know—a painter."

"What's that got to do with it?" Daren asked.

I shrugged. "I don't know that it means anything," I said, "but aren't artists usually considered peculiar?

Maybe not all of them, but the ones we've studied in school weren't very, uh . . . conventional.''

"Hey, that's right," Daren said, "and it's not just artists either. Some of the others, the real creative people like poets and composers, they usually seemed pretty out-of-the-ordinary, too. Eccentric.''

"It still doesn't mean anything, though," I said. "Miss Annie was—is—getting old. Seventy-three, they said. Maybe that's the only reason for her oddness. And it makes me real nervous and sick to my stomach to think that anyone would . . . mistreat an old lady like Miss Annie.''

"If there was something we could do . . .''

But there wasn't anything, and worrying about it wouldn't help either. "Let's talk about something else,'' I said.

"Okay with me,'' Daren agreed quickly. "About our practice today—I've been thinking it's about time we tried the whole course without stopping unless we just *have* to rest. We could get some idea of our time that way.''

I dreaded it. It would be real work, and I doubted that I was ready for that long a stretch, but I agreed to make the effort. "My arms will fall off,'' I muttered, "but we can try anyway.''

When we reached the landing, we were surprised to find another couple there, unloading a canoe. They were from Gainesville High, both seniors. Greg Thomas was a big guy who was a poor student but a popular linebacker, and his partner, Ginger Appleton, looked tiny beside him. She also looked cold and miserable in a bright red bikini. Over it she wore a thin shirt that surely didn't do much to ward off the morning chill. I hoped she had brought sunblock; if not, she'd be suffering from the other extreme soon—sunburn.

"Y'all practicing for the canoe race?'' Greg asked.

"Yes," Daren answered. "You, too?"

Greg grinned, flexing his muscles. "Y'all might as well give it up right now," he said. "Ginger'n me are gonna take first place."

"How long have you been practicing?" I asked.

"Oh, we haven't practiced yet," Ginger replied. "Greg says a couple days training will be enough. He's just so *strong*, you know."

As she talked, Ginger stared first at me and then at Daren, as if she wasn't quite certain what she was seeing. I wondered at her odd behavior, then she cleared it up for me.

"It looks awful strange, seeing you two together," she said. "I didn't know you were . . . uh . . . Are you going together, or what?"

I felt embarrassed, but Daren grinned easily. "We aren't," he said. "We've just suspended the hostilities till after the Riverton Festival. Everything will be back to normal in a couple of weeks."

Although I was amused at Ginger's obvious puzzlement at Daren's explanation, his casualness made me feel even more embarrassed, and I put my things in the canoe and took my seat. I didn't much like the conversation, and I wanted to get away.

Daren joined me and we paddled to midstream, where Daren checked his watch. "Six-thirty exactly," he said. "Are you ready to start?"

I nodded. Greg and Ginger were still on the bank.

I didn't see much of anything then, except the sparkle of the water and my own paddle. Concentration on the paddling took about all of my attention, and we didn't talk at all until we reached the point at which we'd seen the person in the bushes by the field road the day before. I heard Daren say, "Look to the left," and I looked. There on the bank sat Greg Thomas's car; they'd had Ginger's car at the landing where we had seen them.

"They sure don't plan much in the way of training, if they're only going this short distance," Daren said.

"I don't suppose we'll have to worry too much about them beating us," I said, "even though Greg is so *strong*."

"He'll probably run them into the first treetop they come to anyway," Daren said. "Who could keep his mind on paddling, with that red bikini blinding him?"

I grunted in reply, feeling clumsy and awkward in my jeans cutoffs and T-shirt. I heard Daren's low chuckle, and that was all.

On and on we went, with me calling "switch" on every tenth stroke of my paddle. We switched sides smoothly, without breaking our rhythm. Not only did the switching sides equalize the effect of our naturally unequal strength; it also allowed us some rest, since paddling on one side for any real distance put a terrific strain on one arm.

After a while my bottom grew numb, and I felt that I was in some kind of trance, as if my arms would keep reaching, dipping, and pulling back even when I wanted to stop. My mind fell into a daze as well, though my mouth continued saying "switch" on every tenth stroke, automatically.

We passed the Blue Hole, which was the approximate halfway point, and kept on for what seemed like ages, until finally I knew I'd had it.

"Daren, I have to rest," I said.

"I thought you were *never* gonna give up," he groaned. "I thought I was going to have to be the one to holler Uncle."

"How're we doing?" I asked, stretching and relaxing all my muscles. "What time is it?"

Daren whistled. "We're doing great," he said jubilantly. "Wow, I can't believe it; it's just eight-thirty!"

I turned around carefully and sat facing him. "We're about—what? Two-thirds of the way to Willow Bend?"

He nodded, grinning. "If we hadn't stopped to rest, and if we'd kept the same pace, that would mean we did the course in three hours. That's pretty good."

"But we only have eight more days," I said, "and we *did* have to stop. Is it even possible to take an hour off our time in eight days?"

"Sure," Daren said. "We're working together perfectly now, and this is the first time we've concentrated on speed for such a distance. Tomorrow we'll probably make the whole course without stopping, or at least we'll go quite a lot farther than today before we have to rest."

Daren's excitement was infectious, but I still didn't quite share his confidence. On the other hand, I hadn't had any muscle cramps or any other real problems. I had only gotten very tired and somewhat numb. So we weren't doing badly; maybe we could drop an hour in eight days. Maybe.

Our time balanced almost exactly as Daren had predicted. Our rest stop was only for ten minutes, then we went back to the same pace. When we dragged the canoe out at Willow Bend, it was ten minutes until ten. We had only lost ten minutes of the last hour to our tiredness.

"We could start a little later tomorrow if you want to," I said. "At first it took us all morning, but if we can make it in three and a half hours now . . ."

"I kind of like starting early, though," Daren said. "We're the only ones out so early, or almost the only ones. We only see a few people fishing. There isn't anything to distract us this way."

We were standing beside the canoe, just resting for a moment before we lugged it up the slight incline to Daren's car. Daren turned to toss our paddles a little closer to the car, and I saw him pause and stare, and his brows wrinkled in a puzzled frown.

"That's funny," he murmured.

"What is?" I asked, trying to see whatever he was looking at.

"Oh, nothing . . . Guess I parked in a low spot and didn't notice," he said, stooping to lift his end of the canoe.

Then I saw what he meant. We couldn't see the ground over the incline, but the back end of Daren's car was real low. It looked odd that way.

We lifted the canoe, and Daren started up the incline ahead of me. Halfway up, he stopped and stood there, staring.

"What's wrong?" I asked. I was anxious to get the canoe loaded and go home.

His voice sounded so funny when he answered. I heard surprise, puzzlement, and I-can't-believe-what-I'm-seeing all in his voice when he said, "My tires are flat. I've got two flat tires."

We put the canoe down and went closer to see. Sure enough, both of his rear tires were flat as pancakes. They weren't old tires, either; he had just spent two weeks pay to buy them.

We couldn't figure it out. Anybody can get a flat tire, but two at a time is pretty weird. Of course, people did occasionally throw bottles out on the Willow Bend Road, and he could've run over broken glass . . . but two at once?

He wasn't angry then, just irritated, and he fished the keys out of his pocket and opened the trunk.

"What're you doing?" I asked him.

"I'm going to change the . . ." Then he stopped and slammed the trunk lid shut. "I only have one spare," he muttered to himself.

It was funny for a moment, until I remembered how

long and mostly uninhabited the Willow Bend Road was. We didn't really have any choice; one of us was going to have to walk.

"Well," Daren grumbled, "I guess I might as well get started. First house I come to, I'll ask to use the phone and get somebody to come for us. I guess you'd rather wait here, huh?"

That was what I'd been thinking, then I began to feel nervous about staying there all by myself. I was getting as peculiar as Miss Annie, I thought irreverently; until lately, I'd been cautious, but never *afraid* of being alone! What was wrong with me?

"Daren," I said, "what if . . . it wasn't broken glass, or nails, or anything like that?"

He was impatient. "What're you *talking* about, Holly?" he demanded.

"I just thought . . . Well, I know it's silly, but . . . maybe somebody flattened your tires on purpose," I said. I was terribly unsure of myself, and there were butterflies in my midsection all of a sudden.

He practically glared at me for a second, then he began to think it over. "It doesn't make any sense to get two flat tires at the same time," he said slowly. Then he shook his head. "That's crazy, though! Nobody's even mad at me; why would someone do such a stupid thing for no reason?"

I didn't have any answer, but I couldn't shake the eerie feeling that it was no accident. We stood there looking at one another, and finally Daren said, "Well, there's always vandalism—just stupid people who destroy things without any reason."

I nodded. "It could be that," I said. "Anyway, I don't much want to stay here by myself. If it's okay with you, we'll both walk."

"Okay, fine," he agreed. "But we'd better hide your

51

canoe. No use taking a chance on getting it messed up, too.''

So we dragged the canoe into the bushes, put the paddles and binoculars in Daren's car, and started walking.

It had gotten pretty warm by then, with the sun glaring down as if it wanted to burn us to a crisp. Soon we were both perspiring, and the dust from the road and the weeds found its way to our damp skin, somehow. It was stifling. We walked fast at first, then we began to slow down, and it was easier.

It was no big deal, I told myself. Maybe Daren *had* run over two nails, or broken glass had punctured his tires. Either way, he would get them fixed, and a little walk wouldn't do us any harm.

In fact, it might've been almost nice in other circumstances. Walking with Daren might not be the worst thing that ever happened, come to think of it.

Then I remembered what he had said to Ginger earlier about ''suspending the hostilities,'' and I tensed up again. The heat pounded down on us harder than before, and the dust plastered us, and I was more miserable than ever.

Chapter Seven

WE FINALLY GOT home and Daren managed to get his tires fixed, but we had to leave the canoe hidden at the river. There hadn't been time, after that long walk, for us to manage it and for Daren to get to work on time.

Daren called me after work that afternoon. "You're not going to believe what was wrong with the tires," he said. Then he told me. "Nothing. Not a single thing. Someone went to a lot of trouble to let the air out, but there were no punctures. I can't figure out what to make of it."

"It must have been someone's idea of a joke," I said, "although there wasn't much of anything amusing about it."

"You can say that again," Daren said. "If I ever find out who did it . . . It was one of my 'friends,' I'm sure. Probably Brent Thurman; just wait till I see him!"

"I suppose we're going tomorrow, same as always?" I asked.

"Sure. We'll just load the canoe on your truck when you get to Willow Bend," he said. "I hated to leave it there, but it should be safe enough, hidden in the bushes."

"Okay," I said. "See you in the morning."

But I couldn't keep from thinking about those flat

tires. If it had been a practical joke, it seemed a bit harsh of the joker to have flattened both tires. On the other hand, aside from the trouble of that long, miserable walk and fixing the flats and so on, no actual damage had been done. It was very puzzling, but I wasn't getting anywhere by thinking about it.

I left the house on the following morning—it was Thursday—the same as usual, but nothing else about the day was the same. When I got to Willow Bend, Daren had dragged the canoe out of the bushes, and he was bending over it. I got out of the truck and went to help load the canoe, and I saw what Daren had been looking at.

Someone had bashed a hole in the bottom of my canoe!

I was furious, and Daren was angry, too. "This is really going too blasted far," he raged. "The flat tires were bad enough, but this is just plain vandalism!"

"Daren, the canoe was hidden," I reminded him. "This must have been deliberate. Surely it didn't just happen to get found!"

"What else?" Daren asked, throwing a small stone into the water with vengeance. "Yesterday I said that nobody was mad at me; do *you* have any enemies?"

I suppose his suggesting that someone was after me must have stung. Anyway, I blurted an answer without thinking. "I've never had an enemy in my life, except you!" I yelled.

He whirled toward me, his eyes flashing. "Surely you're not accusing me," he said. His face was absolutely frightening.

"No, of course not," I said quickly. "I didn't mean anything; it was just that word—enemy. No, as far as I know, there's no reason for anyone to want to hurt me either. I have no idea who could have done this, or why."

Silently we loaded the canoe, and Daren got into his car and followed me back to my house. We took the canoe into the garage and went to work, patching it.

We worked together, but we didn't talk unless something had to be said. I had put the bad feelings between us again with my thoughtless remark when I was angry and upset, and I couldn't undo my mistake. He knew as well as I did that I hadn't meant to accuse him. What I had done was simply to remind both of us of our years of bickering, just when we'd been on the verge of overcoming all of that.

The patching—not the first patch on my battered canoe—took quite some time. I hadn't done it for a year, and I kept making mistakes. Daren helped, doing whatever I told him, and when we had the job done, it looked awful, but it was watertight again.

We wouldn't be able to use it until the patching had set, so Daren left, with a half-wave and a mumbled "See you."

I didn't blame him for his coolness to me. I felt terrible about having upset both of us, too. We would surely get back to the friendly camaraderie we had shared since our dunking on Sunday, I told myself. Still, I felt depressed by everything. And of course I would have to tell Mom and Dad about the canoe, since they already knew about the flat tires and how we'd left the canoe at the river the day before. When Dad had come in from work, the first thing he'd said was, "Where's the canoe? Did you sink it again?" He hadn't been worried about the flat tires, though; he'd thought it a practical joke, too. But this . . . He probably wouldn't be too pleasant about it.

Still, the rest of the day stretched before me like a barren desert, and I was restless and edgy. I gave the house the most thorough cleaning it had gotten all summer, and still I had time to spend alone. Finally I decided to go to the Spring River Cove, where I could cool off in the water and loaf until Mom and Dad would come home.

The cove was deserted, which pleased me. I felt in no mood to talk to anyone yet. I spread my big towel on the sand, slipped my shorts and T-shirt off and tossed them down, then waded into the cold water. I sat down where the water almost touched my chin, and while I watched, two canoes passed the cove. Tracey Sampson paddled one, alone, and a young couple I didn't recognize was in the other. They were obviously training for the race. They were an unusual couple, because both the boy and the girl had the same shade of red hair. So there *were* others practicing the course; Daren and I had been starting too early to see them before.

After a few minutes I began to feel more relaxed. When I was thoroughly chilled, I went back to the beach towel and stretched out.

The sun felt wonderfully warm and comforting to me then, and my eyelids began to get heavy. I couldn't go to sleep, of course, but maybe just a little catnap . . .

I awoke to the sound of an automobile starting, and I sat up, confused, trying to adjust my eyes to the glare of the sun, which had already brought a stinging sensation to my skin. Then I saw, past where I had parked the truck, a cloud of dust as the automobile sped up the gravel road. All I saw of the automobile itself was a part of the tailgate. I couldn't tell whether it was the same one I'd seen twice before, but it was definitely a brown and white station wagon!

Why hadn't I awakened when the car *arrived*! I was angry and frightened. I couldn't believe I had been so careless and foolish as to actually go to sleep there by the river, by myself. And the driver of the station wagon, whoever he may have been, had surely seen me lying there in my swimsuit!

My knees were weak and my hands trembled as I grabbed up the towel and my clothes, sand and all, and ran for the safety of the truck. I fumbled everything as I tried to start it, but at last I was reassured by the familiar uneven rumbling of the motor. I turned the truck around and started up the road toward home. It was only half a mile, and I had gone about half that distance when I saw the scrap of paper that had been placed under the windshield wiper. I was sure it hadn't been there before.

With my knees trembling again so badly that I could hardly stand, I stopped, and leaving the motor running, got out and took the paper. It was folded, and I didn't look at it until I was back in the truck with the door locked.

I unfolded it. On the paper, in pencil, a message was scribbled: IF YOU KNOW WHAT'S GOOD FOR YOU, STAY AWAY FROM THE RIVER AND MIND YOUR OWN BUSINESS.

I dropped that scrap of paper as though it had been hot, and my hands shook so badly, I was afraid to drive. But I had no choice, and soon I was home, where I felt safe at last. Mom and Dad would be home in an hour.

Mom called about fifteen minutes later. When I heard her voice, I felt so relieved; all day long I had dreaded telling them everything, yet the second I heard her voice, I couldn't wait to tell her and maybe relieve myself of my fear, and what was worse, in a sense, the uncertainty that plagued me.

"Gosh, Mom, I'm so glad you called," I blurted. "I have some really weird stuff to talk to you about."

"You're all right, aren't you?"

"Well . . . sure," I said, finally wondering at the oddness of her tone. It was as though she had called from far away instead of just the other side of Gaines-ville.

"Good," she said. "Now, I don't want you to be upset, Holly, because there really isn't anything for you to be frightened about . . ."

A lot of crazy things can go spinning through your mind in a split second. How could Mom possibly have learned about the scary stuff that had just happened to me? I thought. I hadn't told anyone yet, so how could she know?

But it wasn't that at all.

"Your father's had an accident," Mom went on. "It's only a broken arm and a rather bad headache, but he did fall—the scaffold gave way somehow—and the doctor insists that he stay overnight for observation."

"Stay overnight? Where?" I asked. "And is he *really* okay, Mom? I could come and—"

"That's just it," Mom replied. "You can't. You'll have to stay by yourself tonight, sweetheart, or maybe you could call someone. You see, we're in St. Louis."

"St. Louis! How in the world . . ." St Louis was over a hundred miles away! Dad must be hurt more than Mom was telling me if he'd been taken to the hospital in the city. I shivered, and my arms suddenly felt freezing cold.

"Honey, listen to me and I'll explain," Mom said. "Your father and David Pruitt were standing on the scaffold, and somehow it broke, or . . . Anyway, they both fell. Glenn's left arm was broken, and he took quite a bump on the head. But David was unconscious. They called me, and someone called for the air-evac helicopter from the city, because of David. They wanted your father to come to St. Louis, too, because of the bump on his head, so here we are. I've tried to call you, but you were out. Anyway, your father will be released in the morning. He's fine, I'm sure. At any

58

rate, he's grumbling a lot. And the last we heard, David Pruitt was showing signs of regaining consciousness, so we're optimistic about him as well.''

"But you're sure Dad is okay?'' I asked, trying to force the butterflies in my abdomen to settle down.

"I'm sure. He sends his love, and we'll be home somewhere around noon tomorrow. But he's worried about you, Holly, and so am I. Couldn't you call someone, some friend who'd invite you to spend the night?''

I thought of Rhonda and Jeannie, of course, but they were both out of town. I couldn't seem to think of another single soul I could call, for some reason. Besides, I was no little girl anymore; surely I could survive a night alone.

"I'll just stay here by myself, if it's okay,'' I said. "Tell Dad that I'll lock all the doors and check the windows as soon as I hang up, so he won't worry. I won't leave the house till morning, and I'll be fine.''

"Well . . . if you're sure,'' Mom agreed reluctantly. "Your father said you would want to stay there, but . . . Oh, of course you'll be fine. Gracious, you're practically grown-up! Now, let me give you the number here, in case you should need to talk to us . . .''

And there I was, all alone for the entire night. I was nervous and worried about Dad, and I couldn't sit still. I did make sure the house was all locked up, then I tried to watch television and found that I couldn't concentrate at all.

A broken arm wasn't serious, though. Dad was strong and healthy, and the arm would heal quickly. The worst of the pain would be over by the time he came home, probably. And I knew that it wasn't at all unusual for someone to stay overnight in a hospital when they'd had even the slightest head injury. Surely there wasn't really any need for me to be so jumpy.

Then I remembered the note and the station wagon.

Hearing about Dad had caused me to forget the other thing for a while, and I hadn't said a word to Mom about it after all. For a moment I considered calling the number she had given me, then I knew I couldn't do it. Mom wasn't the nervous type, but I could not tell her something like that while she was so far away, and especially while she knew I was alone in the house. Besides, she had enough to be concerned about as it was. Tough as my father had always been, he could be a real pain when he didn't feel well. Mom had always said that when Dad was sick, he was harder to look after than a child, and she was right. Dad would aggravate her to death. She didn't need any more problems.

I did everything I could think of to keep the crazy scary stuff off my mind. Yet it seemed that the thoughts grew stronger and more frightening every minute instead of vanishing like I wished for them to do.

Even while I watched my favorite comedy on television, a part of my mind conjured terrible images. I couldn't escape it. I heard noises that I had never noticed about the house before, and after dusk, strange shapes flitted past the windows and imaginary intruders rattled doorknobs.

I began switching channels, trying to find something so compelling that I would not be able to take my eyes off it, but in the process, I thoughtlessly paused at channel three. It was a mistake. Channel three seemed always to be broadcasting some horror film. I had never enjoyed that kind of movie even when I personally hadn't the slightest thing to fear.

The few seconds while my eyes watched and before the whole gross scene registered on my brain were entirely too much. I turned the set off.

Then the house was quiet. Too quiet. There wasn't even any traffic on our street. I went to the window and looked out. Across the street, the Montagues' windows glowed invitingly. I could go over and visit with them for a while. That would be a pleasant way to pass the time, and they'd be glad for company. They were always asking me to come over, and I did, sometimes. They were retired, and their children all lived some distance away.

But what if Mom should call? I had told her I would stay inside, and if she called and got no answer, she'd be worried. Besides, if I did go across the street, that would mean I'd have to come back alone, in the dark . . .

I could call Daren, I thought. I needed to call, to tell him about the note. Since we were in the race thing together, the note was surely for him as much as for me.

I had hurt his feelings, and for that reason, I dreaded calling him even though I felt sure that he wasn't actually angry. That in itself was somewhat reassuring, for in the past, he would not have needed any real excuse to be angry—and I wouldn't have cared anyway.

Finally I dialed Daren's number, but there was no answer. Again and again I tried, but neither Daren nor anyone else in his family seemed to be at home.

I was even more alone than I had realized.

Chapter Eight

THE THING WAS, a part of my mind seemed to know I was dreaming, yet I was powerless to end it.

It was horrible. While I watched, unable to walk away, a bearded man in dull green coveralls stooped over the long, narrow box on the riverbank, and lifted the lid completely away. Inside the box lay Miss Annie, in a long pink dress with lace trim at the throat and on the sleeves where they ended at her wrists. Her hands, with long, thin fingers and square-cut nails, rested on her abdomen. On her left hand she wore a narrow gold band, very plain and literally worn thin. On the backs of her hands there were brown spots, yet they looked strong and capable . . . and alive.

Against my will, my gaze moved over her. The box could be nothing but a coffin, and I had never seen a dead person before. Something compelled me to look even when I tried with all my will to turn my head away from her.

In the dream I saw Miss Annie, dead, much more clearly than I had ever seen her in life. Her eyes were closed, and I noticed a little mole on her right eyelid. Though lined, her face seemed almost ageless, as if no number of years having been lived could ever really identify her. Her hair was gray but very pretty, and lay in soft waves about her face. One earlobe showed between the wisps of hair, and a tiny diamond earring sparkled even in the misty early morning light.

As I had done, the bearded man had been standing and looking down at her. Then he straightened, and began to move efficiently. Ignoring my presence as though I were invisible, he replaced the lid on the box and tied a rope around it. The box was already lying across the rope at one end. From that end a long length of rope trailed. I couldn't see the end of the rope.

Once the box was securely fastened and tied, the man stooped and began pushing and shoving, slowly moving the box closer to the edge of the water—to the edge of the Blue Hole. I reached out, wanting to stop him, but I couldn't speak and I couldn't move from where I stood. Powerless, I watched in bone-chilling terror as one end of the box extended over the bank. My horror intensified as the box began to tip, and finally to slide, slowly at first, and then faster until one end touched the water.

There it remained poised for a moment, until the man gave one final shove, grunting from the effort, and the box slid completely off the bank.

At first it sat there, with only a few inches of the box beneath the surface of the water. Then it began to sink, inch by inch.

Suddenly I was freed from my paralysis. I leaped forward, searching for the trailing rope. If I could find it, I could hold on. I could keep Miss Annie from sinking into the inky darkness of the Blue Hole. I could save her . . . . But the box sank, and I could not find the rope, in spite of my frantic searching.

"The rope . . . the rope . . ." I came awake mumbling, sweating, overcome with a terror such as I had never before experienced. The dream was real, so real that some seconds passed before I comprehended that I was lying facedown on my own bed and not scrambling about on the riverbank, trying to find the end of a rope with which I might draw Miss Annie to safety . . .

Fumbling, awkward and frightened, I staggered out of bed and made my way to the shelf where the alarm still buzzed.

It was morning! I had never before been so grateful to hear my alarm.

The nightmare had been so terrifying, so *real*. Ordinarily, the details of my dreams escaped me the moment I came awake, but every fragment of that one remained clearly etched in my memory even after I had showered and dressed.

Soon, however, other things demanded my attention. First, there was my father to think about. Nobody had called, though, and I believed that meant that all was reasonably well. Should I take the canoe and go to Willow Bend? It seemed almost wrong to do so under the circumstances, but I hadn't been able to get Daren on the telephone the night before, and now he was probably already on his way to the river. If I had been thinking clearly, I could have called as soon as I awoke, and told him that I needed to stay at home, but now it was too late for that.

I sat at the table in the kitchen thinking about it, and at last I decided that I would go to the river. Mom and Dad wouldn't be home before noon or perhaps later anyway, and I would surely go crazy waiting if I wasn't busy at something. Besides, it wasn't fair to leave Daren at Willow Bend waiting for me . . . and I wanted to show him the note that had been left on my windshield. We simply had to try to decide what it meant and what we should do about it.

All the way to the river, I couldn't seem to keep from watching the rearview mirror, and it was a relief when I arrived at last to see Daren waiting there beside his old car.

"You're late," he grumbled when he got into the truck with me.

"Sorry," I said. "I couldn't help it. But before we leave, I have something to show you."

I handed him the note, and watched as he read it. Then he looked up, clearly puzzled.

"What kind of foolishness is this?" he asked. He didn't sound too pleasant. Did he think I had written the stupid thing?

"I found it on my windshield yesterday," I explained. "I went to the cove after you left, and I went to sleep on the bank. When I woke up, a car was just leaving. It was that same station wagon. And this note was on my windshield."

"Another stupid practical joke," Daren muttered.

"Do you really think that's what it is?"

"What else? Surely you aren't taking this seriously," Daren said. "Oh, I know it's kind of strange, and if we were still ten years old, it would be scary. But it's just too darned corny to believe—like a thirty-year-old mystery movie or something."

"And what about the station wagon?" I asked, not concealing my irritation. "Can you explain that away, too?" It wasn't that I didn't *want* an explanation. I did. But it seemed to me as though Daren was a little too anxious to shrug it off.

"The station wagon?" he said. "There's just nothing to explain, Holly. Whoever drives that station wagon is free to go wherever he wants, and that includes Spring River Cove, and Tremont Street, *and* the Blue Hole."

"But the note . . ."

"Holly, you didn't see who put the note on your windshield, did you?"

"No, but . . ."

"So why are you so certain it was the driver of the station wagon who put it there? I understand that you've

65

been kinda spooked by that station wagon since the first time we saw it, but you really don't have a thing to base your suspicions on. It's just not fair to be accusing someone of doing things when you don't have any evidence except your imagination. As they say on television, that won't hold up in court.''

And my nightmares won't hold up in court either, I thought as I started the truck. But it didn't seem likely that Daren would put much credence in a nightmare either; better keep that to myself.

I was a little bit worried, a little bit sleepy and tired, a little bit frightened, and a little bit angry, and I didn't say anything else to Daren until we had almost reached Beaver Lodge Landing. Neither of us even thought to turn the radio on. It didn't occur to me in all my irritation that Daren must have been thinking things over a bit more than it seemed.

A little while before we reached our destination, I said, "Daren, I had a bad dream last night. A nightmare." I hadn't even known I was going to say it; the words just seemed to come out of their own accord.

"Yeah?" Daren asked. "A spooky one, huh?"

"I dreamed about the . . . A man was . . ." It seemed so foolish suddenly that I hesitated.

"Well, are you going to tell me, or not?"

"Okay," I said, "but you're just going to say I'm imagining things again. I dreamed that Miss Annie was in this long box, like a coffin. She was dead, I suppose. And this man tied the box up with rope and then he pushed it into the Blue Hole.''

"*That* again!" Daren muttered. "You're going to have to get yourself together, Holly. I never thought you were so . . .''

"So what?"

"I don't know. You've always been levelheaded, I thought. But lately you've been getting some wild ideas.

66

What'd you do, watch a slasher movie before you went to bed?''

I shuddered. "Not likely," I said. "Those things are stupid and disgusting and . . . and just plain harmful. But I was sort of upset. My dad got hurt yesterday. He's in a hospital in St. Louis. But he's okay; he'll be home today, Mom said.''

"Why didn't you *tell* me already, for Pete's sake?" Daren asked. "It's no wonder you're having crazy dreams and stuff. What happened?''

So I told him about Dad, and he was interested and concerned, and I began to feel a little better about everything.

Then we were there, and we unloaded the canoe and I went to park the truck. That's when I found the second note.

It had been written on a brown paper grocery bag and stuck on a little branch by the place where I always parked. There was no way I could have missed it. It, too, had been written in pencil, and it said, GIVE UP. GO HOME AND STAY THERE OR YOU WILL WISH YOU HAD. The most noticeable difference was that the writing was much less legible than that of the first note. It was downright sloppy and almost unreadable.

I was furious, and nauseous, too. I took the paper back to where Daren waited in the canoe. I handed it to Daren and then took my seat with my back to him.

"I sure wish I could get my hands on the joker who's doing this," Daren muttered. "Of course, it isn't necessarily for us. I mean, there's probably a lot of people practicing for the canoe race by now, later on in the day.''

Then he was pushing us away from the bank. For some reason, I had thought he would surely take this more seriously.

"We're going on anyway?" I asked.

"Why not?" he said. "If the note was left there for us, it's just some jerk's way of trying to scare us out of the race, and I'm not going to let something like that stop me. In fact, I'm more determined than ever now. We're going to *win*."

"Okay, if you're all that sure," I said, "but don't be surprised if the windows are broken out of your car when we get down to Willow Bend."

"They'd better not be," Daren said ominously. "I've had about enough of this."

"So have I," I said. Suddenly I felt terribly, overwhelmingly tired. "The truth is, it's beginning to get on my nerves," I said, to myself as much as to him, "and when we get home, I'm going to call the sheriff and tell him about it."

"Fine," Daren growled. "I give up. Call the sheriff. Call the blasted *governor* if you want to, but for now, let's *practice*!"

So we practiced. By the time we got to Willow Bend, I was so exhausted, I could barely drag myself to the car, but we did improve our time. We only stopped once, for about five minutes, and we shaved fifteen minutes off that hour we needed to drop. Daren was excited about that. So was I, but I didn't feel so thrilled as he seemed to be. I was just about too tired to care.

"I told you we could do it," Daren enthused. "We still have seven days to train. I *know* we can get our time down to two hours."

"But two hours might not be enough," I reminded him. "Last year two hours was the winning time, but somebody might be faster this year."

"That's okay," Daren said. He was so confident, I couldn't believe it. "We can get under two hours, if nothing else happens to cost us a day."

That reminded us of the car, that someone was evidently trying to stop us, and we hurried to see whether any other damage had been done.

The car was fine, no broken windows or flat tires, and we loaded the canoe and started home. It was still early, quite a while before noon yet, and I knew Mom and Dad couldn't possibly be at home. Still, I was anxious to be there.

In spite of Daren's certainty that we had nothing to fear, I didn't feel quite so sure. I would at least have to talk it over with my folks when they got home, and I hoped they wouldn't make us stop going to the river. As much as I was nervous and scared, I wanted to continue what we had started. If Daren *was* correct in his estimation of what had been happening, I sure didn't want us to be prevented from our chance at winning the race by some other competitor who simply thought he could frighten us into dropping out.

After telling Daren about my nightmare, I had pretty much forgotten about it. It was only a dream, after all. A dream was nothing to be frightened of, not in the daylight.

I didn't know that the nightmare wasn't over yet.

Chapter Nine

MOM AND DAD got home a little past noon. Dad wasn't exactly in great shape, though he would eventually be well. The broken arm was actually pretty bad, and he wouldn't be able to do any real work for at least three months. Although that would be difficult for him personally, it wouldn't cause any extensive problems, because in a week or so, he would be able to at least supervise his employees in the roofing business. In the meantime, he was supposed to rest a lot and keep the arm elevated and so on.

It was a great relief to have them home, to know that everything would soon be back to normal. And the other man who had been injured was improving rapidly, too, they said.

Dad was grumpy and tired, and he was hungry. But he didn't seem to want any of the food already in the house. Someone had to go shopping.

"I can go to the store," I said. "Just tell me what you want to eat."

It turned out to be a rather long list, and as I drove Mom's car to the shopping center, I grinned to myself. Dad was going to be a real pain for a while, no question about that. But we would manage to keep him busy somehow. In the meantime, I decided to wait until the following day to tell them about my recent experiences.

By then they would be more rested and hopefully they'd be able to offer some helpful viewpoints or advice. I would also leave the decision about calling Sheriff Hooper, who I'd heard had just returned from the East Coast, up to them. If they thought it should be done, I would do it. Away from the river, it didn't seem quite so urgent anymore.

The shopping took quite a while, and I was afraid Dad would be irritated that I had been gone for so long. Yet when I came back to the parking lot, I knew that I would be waiting for a little while longer.

In a parking spot just two spaces away from me sat the old brown and white station wagon. I felt sure it was the same one that I had seen three times before, but it did look somewhat different. It had been washed and waxed, evidently. The other times I had seen it, it had been covered with dust.

This time I would learn something. I took a scrap of paper and a pencil, walked casually around the back of the station wagon, and sure enough, the dent was there. When I copied down the license number, I remembered vaguely that when I had first seen the number in the binoculars at the Blue Hole, they had seemed familiar, and they no longer looked as though I'd seen them before. Yet I was as certain as ever that I was looking at the same automobile.

My insides fluttered a bit as I went back to Mom's car and sat waiting, but I was determined. For once, I would get a good look at the driver. At least I would have some idea of who had been following me. For in spite of Daren's opinion, I felt sure that I had been deliberately followed.

People came and went while I waited. I saw several people whom I knew, but it seemed that nobody would ever come back to the station wagon, and I began to get impatient.

71

Then I saw Mrs. Hooper. A boy who worked in the supermarket pushed a loaded grocery cart for her, and they were coming in my direction. I sat watching, wondering whether I should get out of the car and inquire about their son. I knew it would be a neighborly thing to do, but I was a bit shy. I had never talked to the sheriff's wife before; we had only waved to one another when I mowed Miss Annie's yard.

I had gone so far as to open the car door when Mrs. Hooper and the boy stopped. I watched, stunned, as she took out a ring of keys and unlocked the door of the station wagon!

Nothing made any sense anymore. My thoughts skittered from one thing to another as I drove toward home.

To begin with, the Hoopers owned a beautiful new automobile. I had seen it in their driveway, and I had even seen Mrs. Hooper driving it into the double garage attached to their house. So why was she driving the old station wagon?

I had never actually seen Mr. Hooper, not in person. I'd seen his picture in the newspaper, I supposed, but I couldn't recall what he looked like. Was he a short, chubby man with a beard? Maybe, but I didn't know. Was he the man I had seen, in the flesh and later in my dream, pushing the . . . whatever it was . . . into the river?

Yet . . . the Hoopers were supposedly on the East Coast on the day the station wagon had followed me to Miss Annie's house. Was someone playing tricks, or worse?

I couldn't make sense out of any of it, and in a few minutes I was at home, where I found that Dad had gone to sleep. He hadn't been quite so hungry as he had thought, it seemed.

"It's the medicine—the stuff they anesthetized him

with, I suppose," Mom said. "He hasn't gotten over the effects yet; he keeps drifting off."

"It's going to seem strange having Dad around the house," I said.

Mom agreed. "You'll have to put up with his grumpiness for a while," she said, "but not for long. In a week he'll be spending some time at work, and he won't be so irritable then."

I nodded, and noticed Mom watching me closely. "What's wrong, Holly?" she asked. "I completely forgot until this minute, but didn't you say there was something we need to talk about? Are you okay, honey? You look a bit . . . not quite yourself."

Even while she spoke, Mom stifled a yawn. She was so tired, and I couldn't think of burdening her right then.

"Take a nap while you have a chance, Mom," I said, kissing her cheek. "I do want to talk to you and Dad both, but tomorrow will be soon enough. It isn't urgent. And if I don't look up to par, it's probably all that canoeing. Daren's working me to death!"

She was easily convinced, too exhausted to argue or question me further. Soon she went toward her bedroom, and I hoped she would get to rest for a couple of hours.

I went to the backyard swing to sit and think, but I didn't get very far. Everything had become so confusing. I finally decided that I was absolutely certain about only one thing: whether or not there was any legitimate reason, I was scared.

So what could I do about it? Nothing much, I supposed, except that I could avoid situations where I felt in danger. Reduced to its simplest form, I decided that meant that I must avoid being alone. I felt safe at home, and I felt safe enough even at the river, so long as Daren was with me.

That realization stopped me cold for a moment—that I felt safe with Daren. We had been together each day for only one week, and that time had not all gone smoothly. Yet I felt secure and protected with him anyway. What a remarkable thing that was! I hoped it could continue, that somehow we could manage to be friends even after the Riverton Festival.

But then, of course, perhaps he wasn't interested in our friendship. We had pledged to put our differences aside until the canoe race was over. Maybe that's all it was to Daren, after all.

I shook off such thoughts. They were not my most urgent concern, were they? I had to concentrate on managing two things: continuing the training for the race, but not being alone anymore until something had been settled and I no longer felt so threatened. Maybe Daren was right and I really hadn't anything to fear.

I hoped that was true, but I couldn't quite make myself believe it.

I left the house the next morning as usual, resolved that for the rest of our training time, Daren would come by my house and drive behind or in front of me to Willow Bend, where we would leave his car.

Nothing unusual happened that morning, and Daren was there when I arrived. He agreed without hesitation when I told him that I didn't want to drive alone in the mornings anymore.

There were some interesting comments about Miss Annie on the news broadcast. Since we hadn't listened the day before, we were surprised—and if it hadn't concerned such a serious matter, it would have been an amusing satiric comment on human behavior.

The sheriff's office, state police, and city law enforcement officials were all involved to varying degrees in the effort to learn what had become of Miss Annie. Oddly, she had lived in Gainesville for many years, and only a handful of people seemed to really know her. Miss Annie's friends, it seemed, were from New York City and Philadelphia and Boston . . . and a considerable number had either come to Gainesville or contacted the law enforcement agencies, demanding that she be found. They were impatient with what one called "the small-town, backwoods methods of investigation." They wanted something done *now*.

Daren and I listened spellbound as an internationally known art critic took control of our local radio announcer's "interview" and turned it to suit himself. "The people of your town—your whole *state*—evidently fail to appreciate that in Miss Anne Morgan, you have a national treasure!" he ranted. "She should have been protected, honored, *revered*. Instead, you have allowed some . . . some *hillbilly*, no doubt, to break into her home and . . . and . . ." Here he broke down momentarily, but he regained his composure rather quickly and went on. "Why such a truly *gifted* soul such as Miss Morgan chose to live in such a *bleak, deprived* place as this is beyond me!"

His tirade had given our announcer a moment to prepare. "Miss Morgan explained that very thing to me recently," he said calmly. "She said she couldn't work in the impurity and inhumanity of the city. If you doubt that, it's on tape right here in the studio—"

"Young man, I really do not care for your—"

"So why don't we get on with the subject at hand?" our announcer went on. "I believe I had asked for your expert opinion regarding Miss Annie's early work in oils . . ."

The point, of course, was that a lot of pressure was being exerted, and the law enforcement agencies were stumped. They didn't even know for certain that a crime had occurred, and they were being pressured by some pretty powerful people to solve it.

The final comment on the local news was a simple statement that the person who had robbed the Cedar Hills bank nearly two weeks before was still at large. I had forgotten all about that, but it didn't affect me anyway. Miss Annie, though, that was different. I thought of her dozens of times a day—and more now, since the nightmare.

When we reached Beaver Lodge Landing, someone was there waiting for us. It was the Chester County sheriff, Mr. Hooper. And he was short and chubby, but he didn't wear a beard.

"I'm Daniel Hooper," he said. "You're Daren Peterson and Holly Bennett, aren't you?"

Daren nodded, but the sheriff seemed to be looking only at me.

"Can we help you with something?" Daren asked.

"It's possible," Sheriff Hooper replied. "You've been out here every day for how long? A week?"

"Since last Saturday," Daren said, "except we had to miss one day because of the canoe."

"What about the canoe?" the sheriff asked. I admitted to myself that he seemed pleasant enough and not sinister.

Daren indicated the rough patch. "We had to leave it at Willow Bend overnight," he said, "and someone knocked a hole in it. We patched it, but we had to skip that day while the fiberglass patching dried."

"Why'd you leave it?" Mr. Hooper asked. "Surely you know it wasn't safe. A canoe is too light, too easy to steal, or even to wash away in a flood. You shouldn't leave your canoe at the river." He was still looking at me . . . or maybe I only imagined that, too. Anyway, I kept quiet and waited for Daren to answer.

"I had two flat tires; that's why we left the canoe," Daren said, and the sheriff seemed satisfied with that.

"Have you seen any strangers on the river?"

Daren shook his head. "We've been starting so early," he said. "I guess most people don't want to get out before sunrise, so we have it pretty much to ourselves . . . except . . ."

"Except what?" the sheriff prompted.

I drew in my breath sharply. I hoped Daren wasn't about to mention the man at the Blue Hole, and what must be the sheriff's own automobile! I hadn't told Daren about that yet.

But he wasn't thinking that far back. "There was one day—we didn't exactly *see* anyone, not well enough to know who it was anyhow. But somebody was in the bushes down the river a little way, and I guess he was watching us. Mostly we could just see his legs, though. Other than that, we've just seen a few fishermen."

The sheriff had been watching Daren that time, and when he finished, the man turned back to me. "Holly?" he said.

"Uh . . . I beg your pardon?"

"Have you seen any strangers on the river? You do go down to the cove alone sometimes, don't you?"

I couldn't suppress the shiver that rippled over me, or the sudden rash of goose bumps. How did *he* know that, unless . . . It implied more than I felt able to consider.

"I . . . sometimes," I finally managed. "Once there were some people in canoes, but they were kids—about our age. I think that's all."

He sighed. He appeared relieved rather than disappointed, and I shuddered inside to think what that could possibly mean.

He turned as if to go, then turned back to us. "You two—be very careful, do you hear? The river isn't the safest place to be. Don't let yourselves get careless. Accidents . . . accidents don't always happen to the other fellow, you know."

"We're careful," Daren said, "and we're good swimmers."

The sheriff nodded. "Glad to hear it," he said, "but that's not altogether what I had in mind. The river's dangerous, all right, but not as bad as *people* can be. Stay away from strangers, for certain. There are some people who are . . . who can't be trusted. Remember that."

Then he did leave, and when I was sure that he was really gone, I turned to face Daren, who stared after the sheriff's patrol car with a puzzled expression on his face.

"Boy, do I ever have something to tell *you*," I said.

Chapter Ten

WE SAT ON the riverbank while I told Daren what I had discovered, that the station wagon evidently belonged to the sheriff. For once, Daren appeared to be paying serious attention to what I had to say, although he didn't accept it all automatically. He had a few questions.

"If the station wagon belongs to the Hoopers, why wouldn't you have known that all along?" he asked. "You said you've seen Mrs. Hooper's new car, so why haven't you seen the old one there?"

"They have a double garage, and the doors stay closed," I said. "I suppose the station wagon has been in the garage."

"Then you really believe it has been the sheriff all along?" Daren asked. "Remember, the man at the Blue Hole had a beard."

"Beards can be shaved off," I replied, "and I'm not saying that it was the sheriff anyway. I just think it's possible. He even knew that I've been going to the cove by myself since Rhonda and Jeannie left. Maybe it wasn't the sheriff, but something pretty strange is going on. I do know that much."

"Well . . . look at it this way," Daren mused thoughtfully. "If that automobile does belong to the sheriff, and it really was him that you've been seeing, then it's probably all perfectly legitimate and no crime at all.''

"You could be right, and I hope you are,'' I said, "but there's another way to look at it, Daren. Suppose everything I suspect is completely true. In that case, if the sheriff's involved in something shabby, it's an even *worse* crime than if it were somebody else.''

We went down the river then, and our time was terrific. We managed to shave off another fifteen minutes. We were down to two and a half hours. Both of us were pleased, and when we took the canoe home, we both went in to talk to Mom and Dad.

Dad was sitting in his recliner with his left arm propped up on a pillow. He looked tired and bored, but he brightened when we came in. Daren told him about our progress, and he seemed almost as happy about it as we were. It was fun to see his eagerness.

"You think you might beat Riverton then?'' he asked. "It would be all right if Gainesville could keep the trophy for a year, and it looks like you might have a shot at it.''

"Maybe,'' Daren said, "but Holly and I haven't even had a chance to check out the competition. We really have no idea what we're competing against.''

"Not that it matters,'' I added. "We've been doing everything we could. We couldn't have worked at it any harder. So whether we're ready or not on Saturday, we've done our best. That is, we will have if nothing else happens to interfere.''

"Speaking of that . . .'' Daren paused, looking inquiringly at me. I nodded my agreement, for I knew what he was thinking of. We had more or less decided that we would tell my folks everything, though we still felt hesitant. Did we actually have anything to tell?

Mom and Dad both thought so, though they didn't agree with my fears concerning the sheriff.

80

"But just to be on the cautious side, we'll discuss it with the state police," Dad said thoughtfully. "On one hand, you don't necessarily have a serious problem. No doubt there's a reasonable explanation for everything except the vandalism. But to think that someone has been watching you, Holly . . . that scares me. You should have told us about that before now."

"I guess so," I agreed, "but what if I'm mistaken? Like Daren has been saying all along, it could have been nothing but coincidence. It makes me feel pretty silly even now, to be telling you. But I *have* been scared."

"And now we're scared, too," Mom said. "I know this must be what you've been dreading to hear, but it should be considered just the same. Perhaps you two should stay away from the river for the rest of the week."

I had known one of them would say that, and I was prepared to argue and plead if necessary, but Dad relieved us on that point.

"They've worked too hard to be cheated out of their chance in the race, Patty," he said to my mother. "Aside from the time someone watched from the bank, they haven't actually been bothered on the river. So how about doing it this way: I can't go to work for a week anyway, so Daren can simply come here in the mornings. We'll load the canoe in the truck, and I'll drive them up to Beaver Lodge. Then I'll pick them up a couple of hours later at Willow Bend."

"Hey, that's great!" Daren exclaimed. "Only . . . will you be able to do that? I mean, your arm . . ."

"Sure he can drive one-handed," Mom said, smiling. "He used to do quite a bit of that." She winked at Dad. "Don't discourage him, Daren. It'll give him something to do. Then he won't be such a grouch."

"Listen to that. She's accusing me of being diffi-

81

cult!'' Dad said, grinning. ''What a ridiculous notion. I'm the most pleasant man alive.''

Then we became a bit more serious when Mom said, ''Well, kids, are you ready to talk to the state police?''

The funny thing was that after telling my folks about everything, I felt so much better that my fears had pretty much evaporated. I wasn't so anxious to talk to anybody else then, and when the two uniformed men arrived at our door, I felt embarrassed by the whole thing. Nothing had actually *happened* to Daren or me, after all.

The policemen, however, were interested. They introduced themselves, then encouraged all of us to address them by their first names. I supposed that was intended to make us feel more at ease, but it didn't seem natural.

The young, thin one who never actually smiled was Sergeant Jones. The other, a handsome, graying man who seemed much more comfortable, was Sergeant Leonard.

Daren started at the beginning, when we had first seen the car at the Blue Hole. Then he explained that I had seen more than he had, since I'd had the binoculars, so I told them about that part. And between the two of us, we described everything that had seemed at all out of the ordinary. I still had the notes, and the men wanted to keep them.

They both asked questions to clarify every little detail, and when the sheriff's name came up, I felt embarrassed. I kept wanting to say, ''I'm probably only imagining . . .'' But they were meticulous. They wanted every single detail. Daren, bless his little heart, mentioned that I'd had a nightmare about it, and Sergeant Jones even wanted to hear about *that*. My face felt warm and I stammered a lot, but I told them. When

I was finished, Sergeant Leonard seemed to be smiling. I was sure he thought it was pretty silly of Sergeant Jones to want to hear about the dream, but Jones said, "Thank you for telling us, Holly. Sometimes what we see in dreams can be awfully close to reality." Then I felt a little better about it.

They were thoughtful, then the older man said, "Whether this has any actual connection to Miss Annie is questionable, Holly, but we do know that it's illegal to put junk in the river. So you've done some good anyway, and you mustn't feel awkward about this. I only wish you had noticed more details about that man."

I'd thought my recitation had been quite detailed, and I said so. "What I mean, Holly," Sergeant Leonard said, "is that I wished for the kinds of details you saw in your dream—you know, like the mole on the . . . on Miss Annie's eyelid. But I realize that's too much to hope for. Actually, I think you were very observant."

Sergeant Jones turned to Leonard then. "Maybe she *could* furnish more details," he suggested. "What about the method we used in the Huggins case last spring?"

Sergeant Leonard's brows arched. "That's worth considering, though it's a lot of trouble," he mused. "Still, with all the pressure we're getting . . . How about it, Holly?" he said, turning to me. "How do you feel about being hypnotized?"

"Hypnotized!" Mom exclaimed. "Whatever for?"

"People often recall the most minute details that they had considered forgotten or never even seen, while in a hypnotic trance," Sergeant Jones said. "It's completely harmless when done by a professional. It's also simple and, well, easy, that's all. But some people are rather . . . distrustful of hypnotism."

"I don't know about this," Dad said. "It's completely foreign to me. What do you think, Patty?"

Daren spoke up then. "Holly won't mind being hypnotized," he said with a teasing grin at me. "It won't be the first time, and she's a great subject!"

I blushed, remembering all too clearly the incident to which he referred. It had happened long ago, when we were in the seventh grade. Our whole class had been invited to a birthday party, and someone was there, the host's uncle or something, and he was a hypnotist. He had decided on the spur of the moment to entertain the party guests, and he asked for a volunteer. Daren had called out *my* name, and I'd been too stubborn to refuse. I had gone forward. It hadn't amounted to much. The man had suggested that I was a chicken, and evidently I had clucked and flapped my "wings," and in general made an utter fool of myself with everyone watching. Most of the kids had thought it great fun, but Daren . . . Daren had teased me unmercifully.

"That's right," Mom said, smiling. "I'd forgotten all about that, but Holly *has* been hypnotized before. Had I known about it at the time, I would never have permitted it, but it certainly didn't do her any harm."

If she'd only known! I sent Daren a murderous look for having brought it up, then I said, "It's okay with me, I guess, but who'll do it?"

"There's a woman in St. Louis; we'll look into it and maybe contact her," Sergeant Leonard said. "And we'll also have to get a diver from out of town to look in the Blue Hole. It may take a few days, though. In the meantime, I don't want you to discuss this with anyone, all right?"

Daren and I agreed.

"And another thing . . . It would be wise for the two of you to be cautious. Perhaps there's no actual cause for alarm, but . . . I'd rather have you be safe than sorry."

Dad explained our plans for him to accompany us

then, and the men seemed relieved. I couldn't decide what they were thinking about our crazy story, but they *were* at least planning to investigate it. A part of me felt relief, yet in another way, I was worried. What if I'd started all this for nothing? While they investigated my concerns, their time would be taken from other possibilities. It would be awful if the whole thing turned out to be a wild-goose chase.

But when I mentioned that to Dad, he said, "If you ask me, they were glad to have something legitimate to be doing. I think they were completely out of ideas, and you gave them something to think about."

Whether I had done the right thing or not, I felt a lot more free and relaxed after it was over. I wished for something to do—something fun. It seemed like a long time since I'd done something just for the fun of it.

Daren was still sitting there talking to Mom, and my thoughts had wandered. I hadn't been listening. In fact, I'd practically forgotten that he was there. Then I had a sudden brainstorm, and I said to Dad, "Is it okay if I take the car over to Riverton? I'd like to see a movie or something." Gainesville had a movie theater, too, but they didn't have Sunday afternoon matinees.

"Sure, I suppose it's okay," Dad said, "but you don't plan on going alone, do you?"

I hadn't planned anything, actually. I had spoken without really thinking. I just wanted to *go* somewhere, to relax and not be worried for a little while. But of course, they weren't going to let me go by myself. I didn't even want to, when I thought about it.

"Never mind," I grumbled. "I'll stay home."

"That may not be necessary either," Dad said. "Maybe Daren would like to go with you."

He had only meant to be helpful, but I wished my father had kept quiet. Going to the movies was too much like a date—and who wants a date arranged by her father? I didn't want a date with Daren anyway! In all the time we'd spent together, the subject certainly hadn't come up.

Daren couldn't do much except go along with Dad's suggestion, under the circumstances. He had to be a gentleman in front of Dad, so he said, "Sure. Sounds good to me."

To give him credit, he did smile nicely enough. I knew he probably *wanted* to say, "I'd rather have the measles," but we were stuck, thanks to my impulsive big mouth.

In the car, I tried to apologize. "I didn't mean to get you into this, Daren," I said. "I'm sure you have better things to do than baby-sitting me."

He gazed at me for a moment, and he wasn't smiling. Then he said, "Would you just take it easy, Holly? Surely it won't kill you to spend a couple of hours with me!"

Somehow he had turned everything around, and I couldn't figure out how it had happened. Furthermore, I hadn't the faintest idea what he'd *meant*!

Chapter Eleven

GOING TO THE movie wasn't much fun, because I didn't feel comfortable with Daren. On the river we'd been doing all right, probably because we shared a single goal. But without that purpose, about which we saw pretty well eye to eye, we were almost like strangers. Being real strangers might have been easier, because we had such an unpleasant background that we just didn't seem able to forget.

When we left the movie to go home, we drove through Riverton to look at the decorations. Above the street in the business section of Gainesville, a single wide banner read "LIONS CLUB FESTIVAL, RIVERTON CITY PARK, AUGUST 29." But in Riverton we saw banners everywhere. Those banners named the event the "Annual Riverton Festival," with "Sponsored by Riverton and Gainesville Lions Clubs" in smaller print. The whole town was decked out for the holiday. Stores had signs advertising "Festival week" sales, and drawings for all sorts of things, most of them related to river activities: a canoe, a barbecue grill, a camp stove, and so on. Everywhere we looked, there were reminders of the festival.

It would be exciting to live in Riverton, at least during Festival week, I thought—then I felt bad for having had such disloyal thoughts. It *was* lively, though, and I felt that Riverton kids were fortunate.

"Ever wish you lived here instead of in Gainesville?" I asked Daren, for lack of anything better to say.

He shrugged. "I doubt if there's any real difference," he said. "The towns seem about the same to me."

"It's just the festival, I guess," I said. "I wonder why it's always held here. The river goes by Gainesville, too."

"Because Riverton has the great park. It's even right on the riverbank," Daren said.

Well, it had been a feeble effort at conversation anyway, I thought morosely. I couldn't figure out why I felt so rotten. Surely I didn't really *care* whether or not Daren was enjoying himself. I should be grateful that we weren't insulting one another anymore. Wasn't that enough?

At home that evening, I couldn't read or watch television. Nothing interested me, and when Dad asked me what was wrong, I snapped at him. Then I had to apologize, of course. It wasn't his fault that I felt miserable. It wasn't anyone's fault.

On Monday Dad drove us up to Beaver Lodge. None of us had much to say. I was relieved to have Dad's help, but it felt strange to be in the truck with him and Daren. We listened to the radio, but a lot of static interfered and we didn't hear anything interesting.

"There must be a storm coming," Dad said. "I hope it doesn't spoil the weekend."

"Why do you think we'll have bad weather?" Daren asked. "It wasn't on last night's forecast."

"Because of the static in this old radio," Dad said. "I think it's called electromagnetic radiation. It means some kind of bad weather is interfering with the sound waves, or something like that.''

As we made our way downriver that morning, I decided that my father was probably right. The heat was more oppressive than it had ever been. It seemed as though the very air weighted me down and made the paddling more difficult. Above us, the sky was still a normal summer blue, but it was hard to see clearly for any distance. A haze hung in the air; humidity, I supposed.

But although the heat sapped our energy, we still improved our performance. We were getting stronger all the time, and when we reached Willow Bend, where Dad waited for us, we felt good about our efforts.

Dad said he had been there for some time, and that while he waited, three pairs of teenagers had taken their canoes out there. Apparently they'd just not started as far upriver as Beaver Lodge.

"Those kids may have been training for the race as long as you have," Dad told us. "I think you're going to have some real competition. They looked pretty good to me, especially that red-haired couple. They said they're from Riverton, by the way."

That news didn't exactly cheer us, but we had known that we surely weren't the only couple determined to win. We just hadn't seen much of the others. I felt a little bit depressed about it, but Dad said, "Nobody has worked any harder than you two, I'm sure. And you've been wise to practice the complete course. At least you'll be prepared for the whole distance on Saturday."

I knew he was right, but I wanted so badly for us to win the race. Winning had become more important to me during the past couple of days. I wanted the trophy for Daren more than for myself by then. He had put so much into the training, getting up so early to practice and then working all afternoon at the lumberyard. Daren deserved to win.

Mom had arranged for a couple of days off from work, and when we got home, she had news for me.

"The hypnotist will be here tomorrow afternoon," she said.

My knees grew weak. I wasn't *afraid*, but somehow I hadn't truly believed that the state police would want to follow through with the idea. In fact, I had hoped they wouldn't, because I didn't feel at all sure of myself—and besides, I wasn't afraid anymore.

"Tomorrow?" I said. "Here—in our house?"

"They thought it would be more comfortable for you here, Holly," Mom said. "And I suspect that it's also a way to keep from attracting attention to you—to what you're doing. If they'd asked you to come to the police station, everybody would have wanted to know what was going on."

"I suppose that's something to be grateful for," I mumbled. "I guess if nobody knows about it, they won't be embarrassed trying to explain why they went to so much trouble for nothing."

"Oh, I think there's more to it than that," Mom said. "They did pay serious attention to what you said. Sergeant Leonard is the one who called. He said a diver is coming on Wednesday morning to go down into the Blue Hole."

Again I was surprised. "I hope he finds something," I said. "According to Daren, it was a fish trap. If he's right, they aren't going to feel too good about listening to me, are they?"

"For goodness' sake, will you stop worrying?" Mom said. "Holly, you are exasperating at times! Surely you don't suppose they want to find . . . what you dreamed was in that box!"

"No, of course not," I said. "Okay, I won't complain anymore. I'm not exactly looking forward to it, but I did agree. I'll do it.''

I still didn't feel right. It was a funny feeling, knowing I was about to be hypnotized. I couldn't remember anything much about the time back in seventh grade, except for the teasing afterward. Would I know what was going on, I wondered, or would it be like going to sleep—or dying? And what would I say under hypnosis? I hoped I wouldn't say anything stupid.

"You'll be fine, Holly," Dad said. "Maybe she won't convince you that you're a chicken this time!"

Oh brother!

I tried to put it out of my mind, but it was always there in the back of my thoughts somehow, and I began to want the whole thing to be over with. I couldn't keep from thinking about it on the river the next morning, and we only dropped a couple of minutes off our time, because I wasn't able to keep in the proper rhythm. I was aggravated with myself and I expected Daren to be irritated, too, but he was surprisingly understanding.

"It's not hard to see how you'd be disturbed, Holly," he said. "It must feel pretty weird, about this afternoon, I mean, and the weather has been different, too. Any little thing can throw you off. Don't worry about it; we'll do better tomorrow."

"But this is Tuesday," I groaned. "We only have three more days!"

"We're a great team, aren't we? By Saturday we'll have our time down to ninety minutes!"

I *hoped* we would have three more days. Clouds had been piling up all morning long. If we got a real overnight downpour, the river could be rolling too hard by morning to be safe. For that matter, it might even be raining in the morning. A little rain wouldn't have to stop us if our folks didn't object, but thunder and lightning surely would. We definitely could not be on the river if there was danger of lightning.

We got back to my house long before noon, and Daren came inside with us for a sandwich. I had asked him just to be polite, and his acceptance had surprised me.

After we ate, Dad stretched out in his recliner and Mom was busy dusting the already spotless furniture. I didn't know what else to do, so I said, "Want to go outside?"

We sat on the patio swing and talked about our strategy for the race. We would keep ourselves to the pace that had permitted us to finally cover the whole sixteen miles without stopping to rest, we decided. We would depend on what we had proven to be workable, and if everyone else passed us by—well, we would simply let them go on without attempting to overtake them. Sixteen miles was a long distance to paddle without stopping, but we could do it. Maybe the others wouldn't be able to. We simply had to think of it like that and make the best of our own abilities.

When our plans had been firmly agreed upon, there wasn't a lot more for us to talk about, I figured, but we did talk, and we weren't too awkward about it. He told a funny story about something that had happened at work, and I talked a little bit about my friendship with Rhonda and Jeannie. It felt natural.

When Daren was ready to leave, he said, "I wish I could be here this afternoon, Holly. I mean . . . I wish I could be of help or something."

At first I'd thought he was teasing, but he really did mean it, and I was touched.

"Thanks, Daren," I said, "but I suppose it'll go all right. At least in another couple of hours it will be over with."

"Okay if I call when I get off work?" he asked me. "I'd sort of like to know how it was."

"Sure," I said. "I'll be here."

He turned to leave then. I was still sitting in the swing, and he turned back and stepped closer. To my complete amazement, he reached out and touched my hair.

"You know, I always did like your hair," he said softly. I couldn't reply. I was dumbfounded. He stepped away then and started down the walk toward his car, then paused and half turned. He was smiling, and I could see the old mischief sparkling in his eyes.

"And another thing," he said. "When we were in the seventh grade and we went to that party . . . I thought you were the *cutest* chicken I'd ever seen!"

Now, that, I thought when I was able to think clearly, was the kind of teasing I could take. How in the world had it happened that he was teasing me again, and I knew it was sweet and funny instead of painful?

Mom came outside then. "Looks like rain," she said, looking at the cloudy sky.

"I guess," I replied. I didn't know I was smiling until Mom asked what was funny.

"Oh, nothing much," I said without thinking. "Just . . . men. Do you ever get to where you understand them?"

"What's the matter with you, Holly?" Mom asked, perplexed. "You sure are acting strange. I hope you're not upset about this hypnotism thing. It's going to be just like taking a nice nap, according to the state policemen."

"Oh, I'm not worried about that!" I said. "Let 'em come. No problem!"

I knew she was looking at me like I had just lost my

mind completely, but I didn't know what to say, and finally she went back into the house.

I stayed where I was, looking at the clouds. One was shaped remarkably like Daren's profile.

Chapter Twelve

MISS REYNOLDS SHOOK hands with me as though the twenty years separating us didn't exist. I liked her right away. She sat on our sofa, slipped one shoe off, and tucked her bare foot under her. She was completely at ease in a strange place, not five minutes after she had introduced herself! As soon as Dad had said hello, he'd gone out. He had chosen to kill time in the garage during her visit.

It was remarkably easy to talk to her. She asked me lots of questions in such an interested and lively manner that answering came naturally, and soon she knew all about Daren and me both, about the canoe race and everything.

"So you and Daren have become . . . what? Friends now?" she asked me.

"I suppose so," I told her. "We've stopped our quarreling, at any rate."

"How about the day when you first saw the automobile at the river—the one that you've been troubled about? Was Daren disturbed about it, too?"

And so she led me easily into the subject until I felt ready to mention the hypnosis.

"It's quite simple actually," she said. "A hypnotist doesn't *do* anything to her subject. I'll only be helping you to focus your attention on a specific point in time, excluding all the sights, sounds, and other impressions that affected you that day. Those things tend to clutter your memory, so to speak. With them out of the way, you will be able to concentrate, and you'll recall the most precise details.''

My mother seemed more nervous about the project at hand than I was. "Have you been, uh, practicing hypnosis very long?" she asked Miss Reynolds.

"For more than ten years," Miss Reynolds replied. "I'm primarily a medical hypnotist, but now and then I'm able to assist in investigative situations.''

"Medical hypnosis? What is that?" I asked.

Miss Reynolds took a sip of her coffee and shifted her position on the sofa. By the way her eyes lighted up, I thought she probably enjoyed talking about her work.

"Some people can't tolerate various drugs, such as those that dentists use. Under hypnosis, a patient is completely at ease while the dentist works. The patient feels no pain, and there is no residue of discomfort afterward from the effect of medicines. The dentist's office is just one of several ways that hypnosis can be a real lifesaver," Miss Reynolds explained. "There are many other useful applications as well, such as assisting a person in recalling events, as we'll be doing here today.''

"Will I know what's going on?" I asked.

"Not in the sense that you probably mean," she said. "I'm fairly sure that it will be necessary to induce a deep trance, so it will be like sleeping. Afterward you won't remember anything. But don't worry, Holly. You won't say anything except in response to my questions. The state policemen made it clear enough what kind of information they hoped to gain from this, but they were afraid their authoritative image might interfere with our success, so they suggested that we make a recording of our interview. It seemed to me like a good idea, and you will have the opportunity to hear the recording afterward. So there's nothing at all for you to be nervous about.''

Miss Reynolds was such a comfortable sort of person that I really wasn't nervous anymore. I stretched out on the sofa and relaxed, while Mom sat in a chair across the room, trying to appear relaxed, too.

While I lay there, I heard the rain begin to fall. It began as a shower, but in a few moments it was a torrent lashing against the windows of the living room. I didn't mind the rain at all, though, except for hoping it wouldn't make the river too rough for Daren and me to practice the next morning.

Miss Reynolds sat in a straight chair beside the sofa and began talking softly to me. She suggested that I would grow sleepy, and I did. The last thing I actually remember is hearing her counting backward.

For the rest of what happened, I had to hear the recording. My responses to the first few questions sounded as though I were sleepy or reluctant, then I began answering with more alertness, and it was funny, listening to myself. The most surprising thing was that I sounded so natural. Every time I had ever heard my own recorded voice, it had sounded stiff and awkward. But under hypnosis, my voice was really me. There were hesitant pauses in places, and complete confidence in others. I could even hear a hint of worry or nervousness when I talked about that rectangular box.

As to that, there was something surprising in my report. I had thought the box was five or six feet long, yet under hypnosis, I said it was much smaller. I also described it as solid—not slats of wood as a fish trap would have been—and looking like it was made of

97

metal. A strange and frightening detail was the rope that I had seen only *in my dream.* Evidently I had also seen the rope in the binoculars that day, but I hadn't remembered it. Nevertheless, I described it to Miss Reynolds.

I didn't recall anything terribly revealing about the man, though, except that I described something like a scar on his arm—only I also said it may have been a scratch or even a streak of grease or dirt! I was sure that the state policemen would be thrilled with that "fact."

I had saved the scrap of paper where I'd copied the license number from the station wagon, and when I compared them after the hypnosis session, I was puzzled. My own writing said the license number was NM6394, but under hypnosis, I said it was GHS434. As soon as I heard my own voice reciting those numbers, I knew they were correct. I had been vaguely aware that I'd seen a familiar acronym on that license plate at the Blue Hole, and GHS stood for Gainesville High School. If the number I had copied in the supermarket parking lot wasn't the same, did that mean there were two brown and white station wagons with identical dents in the rear end?

Miss Reynolds talked with Mom and me for a few minutes longer, then she left to deliver the tape. The rain continued through the afternoon. It didn't begin to ease up until almost five o'clock.

Daren called soon after that. I was prepared to tell him about the hypnosis, but he had a different idea.

"Why don't I come over to your house instead?" he asked. "We should drive down to the river anyway and have a look. We need to see how badly the rain stirred it up. Maybe we could stop somewhere for a soda or something, and you can tell me all about what it was like."

I agreed instantly. I couldn't avoid thinking that it was going to be practically a date, and that was really something. Frizz-Head and Jeans on an almost-date! I hadn't been out with a guy since a week or so before we had begun our training, unless I counted going to the movies with Daren on Sunday afternoon. It could be fun, I thought as I slipped into my best shorts and blouse.

I brushed my hair in a useless effort to tame the unruly little curls that were kinkier than ever from all the dampness in the air. Then I remembered Daren saying, "You know, I always did like your hair." I stopped brushing when I thought of that.

He had teased me about my hair for years. Could he possibly have truly liked it all that time? It seemed incredible, but how nice if it was really true!

The rain had all but stopped by the time Daren came, and as I ran out to his car, I caught only a few sprinkles.

"Hi," he said. "You don't *look* like you had a rotten day."

"It's been pretty nice, come to think of it," I replied. "The hypnosis wasn't bad at all, and she was the *nicest* lady! But I don't think I told them anything useful, just a few things to puzzle them."

"Like what?" he asked.

So I told him about the license numbers not being the same, and about the discrepancy in the size of the box and so on, and he thought it was funny. But even Daren couldn't find anything amusing about that rope that had appeared in both my dream and the hypnosis memory.

"I think that's downright spooky, that there might be—probably *is* stuff in my mind that I don't even *know* about," he said.

I agreed. "It was odd, all right," I said. "But aside

99

from that, if there really is a rope, what in the world would it be for? That's what I can't figure out.''

''Well . . . to tie the box somehow, I guess,'' Daren said, his eyebrows puckered in a thoughtful frown. ''That's what a rope is for, after all.''

''But you can't tie things underwater,'' I said. ''Not unless you're underwater, too, that is. And that man stayed on the bank and pushed the box in.''

''Then what?'' Daren asked. ''Just pretend you're hypnotized and tell me everything.'' He was smiling.

''Then he got into the car and left,'' I said. ''But before he pushed the box in, he was out of sight almost, for a minute. Maybe he was sitting on the ground, or kneeling, or something.''

''Yeah, maybe he was tying that rope to something,'' Daren said.

''Daren, I think you've got it!'' I cried. ''That *must* be what he was up to. Why else would he have even had the rope?''

''I wish it wasn't so nearly dark,'' Daren said. ''We could drive down to the Blue Hole and have a look from the bank. Maybe we'd see something.''

''No need, though,'' I said, shivering at the thought. ''The diver's coming tomorrow. Let him do the looking.''

We found the river muddy from all the rain, but it hadn't risen to the point where it would be dangerous for us in a canoe.

''Don't count on it yet, though,'' Daren said. ''If the rain came from the north, the river could still rise a lot before morning. We'll just have to wait and see.''

So he'd known all along that we wouldn't be able to tell anything by looking at the river, hadn't he? That meant that he'd *wanted* to go somewhere with me. I

100

didn't know how to feel about the idea, although it did give me a couple of goose bumps. Did I want Daren to like me, or what?

We went to the busiest fast-food joint in Gainesville after looking at the river, and we saw lots of Gainesville kids. They were all talking about the festival and hoping it wouldn't get rained out. Most of the girls were all giggly and oh-so-modest about the beauty pageant, and about their fabulous dresses. It was funny to listen to. One way or another, the girls would find a way to mention how much they'd paid for their pageant dresses.

Then I scolded myself for being hateful. If I'd been interested in entering the pageant, I'd probably be talking just as silly as they were. As it was, I was more interested in the talk about the canoe race.

"Greg says he and Ginger are gonna take the trophy," Bobby Ryan said. "How about it, Daren? Think he can do it?"

"Be at Willow Bend on Saturday morning," Daren replied with a grin. "You'll see who comes in first."

"Oh, we'll be there, all right," Bobby said. "But not to see who wins the canoe race. What we want to see is you and Holly back to normal! What time will the fun start, do you think?"

I felt like throwing my soda at Bobby, but Daren only shrugged. "Guess you'll have to wait and see about that, too," he said. "We wouldn't want you to miss anything."

We left the restaurant then, but Daren didn't start back toward my house right away. Instead he seemed to be driving aimlessly. We weren't talking, but it didn't feel too uncomfortable.

Finally I decided we might as well get it over with. "You and I must have been terrific entertainers all these

101

years," I said. "They can't leave it alone, can they? Everybody wants to see us fighting again."

"I guess we *were* worse than I realized," Daren said. "I really . . . . gave you a hard time, didn't I, Holly? I wish I hadn't done that."

"You aren't a bit more to blame than I am," I said breathlessly. "I tried very hard to give as good as I got. How'd I do, anyway? Was I what they call a worthy adversary?"

Daren flashed me a wide grin. "About as 'worthy' as they come," he said. "You were tough. You wouldn't believe how much time I spent on trying to outdo you. I *worked* at it, Holly, at finding a more cutting insult."

"So did I," I admitted. "It's hard to believe, isn't it? That we invested so much time and energy into hurting one another. Daren, I want you to know that I wish I'd been different . . . except . . ."

"Except what?" he asked me.

"Except . . . it *was* kinda fun," I said, surprising even myself.

Daren laughed aloud. "Yeah, it was at that," he said, "except for the times when I thought that I really *had* hurt your feelings. Then I always felt rotten, but I'd have died before admitting it."

We were quiet for a while then, just driving around town, without any real purpose except to put off going home for a little while longer. I felt as light as a feather, almost giddy with happiness. We had finally actually *talked* about all those years of bickering, and we'd done it in a way that didn't hurt at all. Maybe now we would be able to put it behind us and be real friends.

Finally I said, "I wish we could watch the diver in the morning. Wouldn't you like to be there when he finds out what the box is, Daren?"

102

"It may not be there any longer," Daren said. "Maybe whoever put it there has already taken it out. I mean, it *must* be something he'd want to retrieve, if he's tied it somehow with a rope."

"Doesn't matter anyway," I said. "We can't afford to waste a day of training. The diver and those nice policemen will just have to get by without us."

"Yeah, unless the river's too high in the morning," Daren said. "Well, I guess I'd better take you home, Holly. Your Dad'll think we've eloped or something."

"See you in the morning," I said at my front door.

"Yeah, okay. See you," Daren said. "Good night, Holly."

"Good night, Daren," I said.

It sure was a humdrum way to end the nicest evening of my entire life!

I didn't get much of an opportunity to savor my enjoyment, though, for I hadn't been inside the house for more than five minutes when the telephone rang. I answered it.

"Are you Holly?" a harsh male voice asked.

"Yes I am," I said.

"You've caused me a lot of trouble, girl," he said. "You've been talking to the cops and meddling in things that you should have left alone, and you're *going* to be sorry."

Then he hung up.

I couldn't believe what I had heard. There was no way it could have been a joke that time, for the voice was certainly that of a man; it was none of Daren's or my friends, for certain.

I stood there by the phone, and I couldn't seem to move. I must have been thoroughly stunned, because Mom had to speak to me twice before I could get my wits together enough to comprehend what she was saying.

"Holly, what is the *matter*?" she cried. "Who was on the telephone?"

I looked at the receiver still in my hand, and finally replaced it. "I don't know," I said to her. "It was a man. He said I would be sorry for talking to the cops and causing him a lot of trouble. He sounded mean and . . . scary."

Things were pretty radical for a while after that. Dad called Sergeant Leonard, and he said he would be right over. Then I called Daren, who said the same thing.

Mom made a pot of coffee, and I noticed that her hands trembled when she took cups from the cabinet. I felt pretty shaky myself, but in only a few minutes, Daren and Sergeant Leonard were both seated at the kitchen table with Mom and Dad and me.

I was able to tell them exactly what the man had said, but I couldn't tell them anything about who the caller might have been.

"Are you sure it wasn't the sheriff?" Daren asked me.

I nodded. "It wasn't his voice," I said. "I know it wasn't him."

Sergeant Leonard spoke up. "We've just cleared up the sheriff's part of the mystery, thank goodness," he said. "Thanks to that license number you recalled under hypnosis, we know that the sheriff's station wagon and the other one you saw were the same, but the ownership has been transferred. Sheriff Hooper sold his new car. You know about his son's accident? He's getting money together to pay for the boy's surgery. Anyway, he bought the station wagon from a used-car lot in Riverton, on the same day he and his wife returned from the East Coast."

"That explains why it was so much cleaner when I

saw it at the supermarket," I said. It was a relief to know that the sheriff evidently wasn't doing anything wrong.

"But who owned the car before the sheriff bought it?" Daren asked. "Surely you were able to learn that, too."

"Yes, but it isn't helpful, because the station wagon has been on the car lot for a couple of months," the policeman said. "The previous owner simply didn't remove the old license plate when he sold the station wagon to the car lot."

"Do you have *any* idea what's going on, Sergeant Leonard?" Dad asked. My father's voice was still strong, but I felt that I could hear a touch of fear in it just the same.

The sergeant scratched his nose and moved uncomfortably, but finally he answered.

"I'm not at all certain," he finally said, "but I have some idea. I believe it does have something to do with whatever's in that box in the Blue Hole. You see, we already made some effort to recover the box, with grappling hooks. But we didn't find it. And since then, we've had a man watching the place."

"So you think . . . the man who called and threatened Holly is mad because he can't retrieve the box now?" Daren asked. "Wow! That means there really *is* something . . . But what could it be?"

"Hopefully not what I dreamed, at least," I said. "According to when I was hypnotized, the box isn't as big as I thought. It's not big enough to have a . . . a body in it." I didn't mention the thing that continued to torture my private thoughts about the box—that if a human body was dismembered, the container wouldn't have to be as big as a coffin . . .

Mom hadn't said much. She looked awfully pale and scared, but at that, she spoke up.

"The only thing I'm *sure* of," she said, "is that Holly isn't going on that river tomorrow. I don't *care* about the canoe race anymore. I'm afraid for my daughter."

Chapter Thirteen

MOM'S INSISTENCE TOOK care of Wednesday for us, but I didn't mind. I wasn't all that eager to go on the river anyway, after the phone call. What really did aggravate me was that they wouldn't let me go to watch the diver at the Blue Hole either. Dad and Daren went together, but they made me stay at home!

"Suppose that man, whoever he is, is watching," Dad said. "He already blames you for spoiling his plans, and there's just no sense in taking a chance on letting him *see* you there, too."

"We'll tell you everything, Holly. I promise," Daren said. He did look unhappy for me, but he agreed with my father just the same.

I knew their caution made sense, but I still wanted to be there, and when Dad and Daren returned a couple of hours later without having learned anything, I thought it served them right. At least I thought so at first.

"The river was simply too muddy from the rain," Dad said. "The diver tried, but he couldn't see, and he didn't find anything. There were so many tree roots running out from the bank that it was too dangerous to be diving in that muddy water."

"So will he try again later?" I asked.

Dad nodded. "The water patrolman said it should be clear by Saturday," he said.

"But that's—"

"Yes. The day of the race," Daren said. "And that's creating a bit of a problem." It wasn't until he said that, that I noticed how serious and troubled my father appeared.

"Patty, we've got to have a talk," he said to my mother. "Let's all sit down. Daren, you explain about Jerred Grayson."

"Jerred Grayson? Who's that?" I asked. "I've never heard the name, I don't think."

"I know," Daren said, "but if Sheriff Hooper's suspicions are correct, you've heard his voice."

"Then the sheriff knows who it was, the man who . . . ?"

"Jerred Grayson lives in a shack in the woods not far from Cedar Hills, and he worked in the body shop at that used-car lot in Riverton for several weeks. That's where the sheriff saw him," Daren said. "He fits your description of the man at the Blue Hole. He even has a bad scar on his arm. The thing is, he's mentally . . . disturbed. He started making threats about how he was going to hurt a lot of people, and the owner of the car lot fired him on the same day Sheriff Hooper bought the station wagon."

"Why was he threatening to . . . hurt people?" Mom asked in a shaky voice.

"Because they sold the station wagon, evidently," Daren said. "Or rather, that seems to have been the breaking point. The owner had been letting him drive it sometimes, and somehow the guy had gotten it into his head that the car was *his*. The sheriff says they knew that Grayson was unbalanced, but he usually behaved pretty normally. But after they sold the station wagon and the sheriff had gone, the man just blew up. He went off the beam completely. Until then, the guy at the car lot had felt sorry for him—and besides, he was a good worker—a good body man."

"So why doesn't someone simply go and arrest him?" Mom asked.

"In the first place, nobody knows for sure that he has actually committed any crime," Dad explained. "But they would arrest him anyway, for the threats . . . if they could find him."

"And . . . the problem concerning the canoe race?" I asked, wishing that my insides would settle down so I could breathe more easily.

"They can't cancel the festival," Dad said. "Too many people from all over have entered the competitions. But they're very much afraid that this Grayson might cause some real mischief that day. And with the crowds of people who'll be there . . ."

"What it amounts to is this," Daren said. "Since he has specifically threatened you, you'll have to stay away from the festival."

"But that's not fair!" I cried. "We've worked so hard; it's just not a bit fair."

Everyone was quiet for a little bit, then Dad cleared his throat. "Sergeant Leonard mentioned another possibility," he said.

"We could go back to the river tomorrow and Friday, and practice for the race just like before," Daren said quietly. "Only there'd be a few . . . changes. We would wear bullet-proof vests under our life jackets. And two water patrolmen would be following us in a canoe of their own. Also, at intervals along the river, the sheriff's deputies and other law enforcement people would be hiding on the bank, or posing as fishermen in boats."

"No!" my mother cried. "It's too dangerous!"

My father held Mom close. "If he isn't caught soon, there's no telling who might get hurt, Patty," Dad said softly. "The whole idea makes me sick, but I can't stop thinking about what might happen at the festival with that madman running loose and planning to punish the world . . . all the little children . . ." His voice trailed off then.

While my father talked, I had been thinking. The proposed plan had me scared silly just from talking about it, but the things Dad had said made a lot of sense. That crazy man could get it into his head to do just about anything, if he was convinced that the world was against him. But if he specifically wanted *me*, maybe it would be worth it to go to the river and be . . . bait. But there was something else on my mind as well.

"Mom," I said, "what if they don't catch this Jerred Grayson, and what if he *doesn't* show up at the festival—he'd still be after me, seems like. I wouldn't even be able to go to the store by myself, or . . . or anything. I'd be scared out of my mind all the time, and the law can't protect me forever. At least if I take this chance, I'll have some protection."

"That's the point Sergeant Leonard made," Daren said, "but we sort of thought we'd just . . . let you think it over for yourself."

"I guess we were almost hoping that you'd refuse point-blank," Dad added.

Mom was all but crying outright by then, but how could any of us comfort her? What we were discussing was dangerous; there was no question about that. The only question was which would be more dangerous: deliberately exposing myself to a man who wanted to hurt me, or taking the chance of waiting to see what would happen and being a prisoner myself until something did? Scared as I was, the first approach seemed preferable to the other one.

Dad told us about Sheriff Hooper then. As soon as they had learned that his ownership of the station wagon didn't mean anything, the state police had told him everything I'd had to say—except that I had actually sus-

110

pected him. That had provided the break that was needed, since the sheriff knew a little bit about Jerred Grayson already. He had been quick to follow through on the investigation then, but it was already too late. Grayson had disappeared.

It was nearly noon, and Daren had to go to work. That left Mom and Dad and me alone. Before the afternoon was over, we would have to make the final decision and call Sergeant Leonard, who would be ready to set the plan in motion as soon as we let him know. Daren had simply said, "Whatever you want to do, Holly, I'm with you." They all wanted me to make the actual decision.

We were all restless, and Mom began dragging all the stuff out of the hall closet. When she was worried, she cleaned things.

Dad was just as bad. "The grass needs cutting," he said. "I think I'll do it now."

"The lawn mower blade has to be sharpened first," I said, "and you can't do that with one hand."

"I can if you'll help me take it off," he said.

So we went outside, and I took the wrench out of the toolbox. We removed the blade and took it into the garage. Dad held it against the grinder, somewhat unsteadily with one hand, and I wondered whether he had actually sharpened it any. Then I helped him put the blade back on.

Dad opened the little toolbox to put the wrench back, and he said, "What's this, Holly?"

I turned to look, and saw that he was holding the scrap of paper I had picked up in Miss Annie's yard several days before.

"Oh, that's nothing," I said. "Just a piece of paper. I picked it up in Miss Annie's yard last week."

He studied it for a moment. Then he said, "This is the carbon of an airline ticket, Holly!"

"Sure enough? I've never seen an airline ticket before," I said. "Let me see it."

"No, that's not . . . What I mean is, this looks like it hasn't even expired yet. You don't suppose . . . Surely if Miss Annie went off on a trip somewhere, Sergeant Leonard and the others would have been able to learn that!"

Then I began to see what he meant, and for a couple of seconds it was an exciting possibility. Then reality set in. "If *anything* in the movies is believable," I said, "there's just no way at all that she could have used that airline ticket without the police finding out about it. Surely they could have learned that with a couple of telephone calls."

"I'd better call Sergeant Leonard anyway," Dad said. "Or, on second thought, I'll deliver it to the station instead. I'd be happier if no more policemen in uniforms showed up here. No point in making it even more obvious that we're talking to them. Will you, uh, be okay? Maybe you could just stay in the house while I'm gone. Help your mother with the cleaning or something."

That remark of Dad's made my decision for me. If he was starting to suggest that I should hide myself already, it probably wouldn't be getting any better in the near future.

"Dad," I said, "I've decided. When you get to the station, would you tell Sergeant Leonard that Daren and I will be going to the river tomorrow?"

Dad looked more troubled than ever. "Holly, are you sure?" he asked. "Maybe you should give it a little more thought before you commit yourself to this."

I shook my head. "I'm going to do it," I said. "I don't want to think about it anymore."

"Well, all right," he said reluctantly, and finally he left.

Mom was almost silent for the rest of the day. A couple of times I started to say something foolish, like, "Mom, I'll be all right. Nothing is going to happen to me." But I didn't feel all that certain. I was afraid, and I felt glad when Dad said Daren would be coming over after work.

As to the airline ticket, Dad said they would look into it, and that was all there was to that.

Then Daren came, and we sat in the patio swing. The only thing on our minds was what might happen the next day, naturally.

"I wish we'd never started this whole canoe race thing," Daren said. "It was supposed to be fun, but now we're in a real mess."

He was worried about me, and I was touched. I wanted to put him at ease some way, but I didn't know how, so I resorted to teasing.

"If we hadn't started it, I'd still be calling you Jeans and looking for new 'ugly' jokes," I said.

"Well, I don't mind admitting that I'm glad *that's* over with," he said with a good effort at a smile, "but given a choice, I'd rather be swapping insults and know that your life wasn't in danger."

Just then we heard a car approaching, and I said, "That's probably the guy Sergeant Leonard's sending over with the bullet-proof vests for us. Doesn't all this make you feel like you're acting in a cops-'n'-robbers movie?"

"How can you joke about it?" Daren asked. "I'm scared, Holly. I'm scared for you especially, but the truth is that I'm just plain afraid for both of us!"

"So am I, Daren," I said. "Don't let my feeble joking fool you. I'm not looking forward to this adventure one bit."

We heard the car slowing down, and we watched with interest. The man who would instruct us about

113

the safety equipment and the procedure wouldn't be wearing a uniform, and we wondered what he would be like.

Then the car came into view, moving very slowly. But it didn't turn in at our driveway. We couldn't see a thing about the driver, with the late afternoon sun reflecting off his window, and when it passed the driveway, it speeded up and went on down the street.

Dad stuck his head out the door. "You two get inside," he growled. Apparently he'd been watching the car from the living room window. Until he said that, it hadn't even occurred to me to be afraid of a passing automobile! When the reason for his concern dawned on me, I was even more glad that I had decided to go on with Sergeant Leonard's plan.

A young man arrived a little while later, carrying a plain cardboard box. He showed us the vests then, and made us put them on. We even had to make sure that our life jackets would zip over them properly. They were surprisingly thin, but wearing them would still interfere with our paddling the canoe.

When I said that aloud, Mom said, "For goodness' sake, Holly, stop worrying about that race! You promised me that you would concentrate on your own safety tomorrow!"

"I will, Mom. You can depend on that," I assured her. "But I figure that we'd better look like we're training as usual tomorrow. That's all I meant."

She relaxed a little bit then, but not very much. After the young man had told us what to expect on the following day, he left, and Daren had to go home soon afterward. He had told his folks everything by then, and they wanted him home early. They were worried, too.

Then there was just the three of us, and it was the most uncomfortable evening I could remember ever having experienced. I was glad when bedtime came, although I felt pretty certain that there wouldn't be very much sleep for any of us that night.

Chapter Fourteen

"TRY TO FORGET what's really happening today," Daren said as we pushed off from the ramp at Beaver Lodge the next morning. "Pretend that this is an ordinary day if you can."

"Not a chance," I said, "but I will try to keep from thinking about Jerred Grayson, who could be hiding behind one of these rocks or trees, ready to attack at any moment and do goodness-knows-what."

"I don't think you're approaching the project of 'forgetting' in quite the right way," Daren said, flashing me a quick grin. "But honestly, Holly, with all these guys who're supposed to be watching out for us, we should be safe enough."

"I just hope something does happen," I said. "That is, if he's going to do anything, I'd like to get it over with. It's the waiting, the not being certain, that's getting on my nerves. Daren, do you realize that Jerred Grayson might even have left the country? I'm afraid of every shadow, and he could be in Canada by now."

We had been instructed not to pay very much attention to the two men who arrived and unloaded a canoe a couple of minutes behind us, but I couldn't resist taking a look. One was young; he looked almost like a teenager. The other man was older, with gray curly hair. They were dressed in ordinary clothes, not in swim trunks or shorts, which I thought would have been more natural. They put an ice chest and a plastic bag half-full of something in the canoe. I wondered about the contents. They looked innocent enough. They could have been any father and son out for a day of loafing on the river, and I didn't think anyone would be likely to suspect them of being water patrolmen.

Other "fishermen" would be putting boats in the river at different access points as we went downstream. It would look too suspicious if the same two men followed Daren and me the whole way, they had said. Others would be keeping an eye on us as well, but we probably wouldn't see them.

Spring River had always been a popular place for fishing, and Daren and I had seen from one to three or four fishing boats every day we'd been out. On that day there were a few more boats and canoes than usual, and the occupants tended to be a little younger on average. Other than that, there wasn't much difference.

After some time passed and nothing out of the ordinary had happened, I began to relax in spite of the peculiar circumstances. Daren and I paddled hard. Since we had to be there, we might as well make the most of it, he had said. We could still win the race—if things went right so that we'd actually get to participate.

At the access point where someone had watched us from the bushes that day, I saw two men standing on the bank. They didn't pay any attention to us. I thought one of the men was my father, but I didn't look very carefully to see. The cast on his arm would have identified him, but he stood sideways, so I couldn't tell at my quick glance whether it was there or not.

A little farther downriver, we were badly startled when a canoe painted in camouflage seemed to pop out in front of us from nowhere. My chest seemed to be encased in lead suddenly. I could barely get my breath when I saw that the man in the canoe had a heavy, dark beard.

Then I realized that he was very tall, and I drew a deep, shuddering breath. It wasn't Jerred Grayson after all.

After that, the trip went smoothly except for my tension. At some point that I wasn't aware of, the two men following us in a canoe were replaced by one man in a small boat, and the boat had disappeared by the time Daren and I reached Willow Bend. My father was there waiting for us, and Mom was with him. It was a great relief to see them both, but I resisted the urge to rush into their arms. If anyone suspicious *was* watching, it would look a bit strange to see such an emotional reunion after less than a two-hour separation.

We went home then, and Daren stayed until it was time for him to go to work. We didn't have much of anything to say to one another, for both of us were depressed by then. Still, it was comforting to have his company.

I didn't feel like doing anything at all, but I had promised to mow two yards. The promise had been made several days before, and Mom wanted me to postpone both jobs, until she realized how irritable I was. Then she changed her mind.

"Glenn, go with Holly to mow those yards," she said to Dad. "Surely nobody could know about that. She'll be safe, but you go along just in case . . ."

So we loaded the lawn mower, and I was glad after all, to have something to occupy the afternoon. *Thinking* about Jerred Grayson's threats was beginning to make me ill.

We didn't get home until almost three-thirty, and I went inside to make Dad a glass of tea.

"Sergeant Leonard called," Mom said. "He left a message for you."

"What now?" I asked, dispirited. "Some new plan for me, since the first one didn't work?"

"Not exactly," Mom said. "As to that, he asked me to convey his appreciation for your cooperation, and Daren's. He said his men reported that the two of you followed the directions precisely, and they're proud of you. So much so that they want to do exactly the same thing tomorrow, except that his men will exchange places so they won't be conspicuous. I tried to talk him out of it, but he wanted to leave it up to you again. What do you think? Was it very bad this morning?"

I shrugged. "It wasn't the best day of my life," I said. I just couldn't seem to feel positive about anything.

Dad came in then and heard what I had said. "At least the practice was good," he said. "You dropped a couple more minutes off your time today."

Mom glared at him, then turned back to me. "Sergeant Leonard said that you must watch the television news at four o'clock. He said there will be something on the news that you will definitely want to see. I was afraid you'd be late."

"He didn't tell you what it's about?" I asked.

Mom shook her head. "It's only thirty minutes," she said. "Whatever it is, we'll all know in a little while."

I hadn't the slightest idea what to expect, but I put a new cassette in the VCR. If it was something I would be particularly interested in, maybe I'd want to keep it.

The news anchorman said, "The majority of our lead stories on the evening news tend to concern violent or fearful events. Tonight all of us rejoice at the opportunity to bring you good news instead. Miss Anne Morgan, nationally known artist, has been missing from her hometown for two weeks, and it was feared that she had met with some tragic fate. That fear has now been

119

put to rest, thanks in part to Miss Holly Bennett, sixteen-year-old resident of Gainesville, who provided the clue which led authorities to the deserts and mountains of New Mexico, where news correspondent Riley Conover talked with Miss Morgan early this afternoon.''

The scene shifted to a stark landscape of granite mountains silhouetted against a cloudless sky, and I watched in dumb amazement as the camera's focus came to rest on Miss Annie, wearing rumpled slacks and an old wide-brimmed hat, and a young, handsome man with a microphone.

''Miss Morgan, were you aware that the people of your hometown, not to mention hundreds of your friends and associates from the art world, have thought for about two weeks that something terrible had happened to you?'' the newsman asked.

''I didn't know it until you told me,'' Miss Annie replied in her brusque, no-nonsense tone. ''Can't a person take a little trip anymore without making a public announcement? And why would they assume I'd been kidnapped or murdered, anyway?''

''Because your front door lock was broken, and someone found your house in some kind of disorder. And there was some blood in your kitchen sink, so I understand.''

Miss Annie, hands on her hips and glaring at the young man, said, ''That lock has been broken for a month, and I did it myself. I accidentally locked myself out one day. I had to get back in some way, didn't I?''

''Then you came out here, over a thousand miles away, without having your lock repaired?'' he asked, clearly incredulous.

It was a marvelous comedy for anyone who knew Miss Annie, but I did feel a little bit sorry for the young reporter. Miss Annie looked at him as though he were somewhere near two years old. "Nobody would *dare* bother my house," she said. "Sheriff Hooper lives right next door, and that makes my house about the safest place in the world, next to the inside of the county jail itself."

"But someone evidently did enter your house, ma'am . . ."

"Yes, and I'll bet you ten dollars it was Daniel Hooper!" Miss Annie said. "It didn't occur to me that the *sheriff* might come snooping around."

"But Miss Morgan, what about the blood?" the reporter asked. "And the dresser drawers that were left open?"

For the first time, Miss Annie appeared somewhat abashed. "I thought I'd cleaned that up," she said. "Maybe I'm getting a bit forgetful after all. I had to look everywhere for my airline ticket, and I guess I left things in a mess. And I cut myself, on the same evening that I left. See?" And she indicated a faint pink scar on her left hand.

"I see. And you're here in New Mexico now, studying . . . ?"

"I'm here *looking*, that's all," Miss Annie said. "I wanted to see some of the country that influenced the artist Georgia O'Keefe's work before I got too old to travel."

The young man nodded his head as though to indicate that he understood, but I felt pretty certain that he was completely confused and dumbfounded.

"One more comment, if you don't mind, Miss Morgan," he said. "Perhaps you have some message for all the people who have been so distressed about your absence? Their concern *is* quite a tribute, don't you think?"

Miss Annie nibbled at her lower lip for a second, and as she moved her head, I saw for the first time that she really was wearing tiny sparkly earrings. They looked like diamonds.

At last Miss Annie responded to the young man's question. "Well, you said that Holly found the clue that led you to find me," she said. "I *am* glad that she cut the grass. At least *one* of my friends didn't have me dead and buried yet!"

I blushed a little at that, remembering how I had hated mowing her yard when I really did think she was dead. Then I wondered: If Miss Annie was as healthy and as grouchy as ever out in New Mexico, *what was in the box in the bottom of the Blue Hole*?

Mom was laughing for the first time in a couple of days, and Dad wore an amused grin, too. But what must all the authorities who'd been frantically searching for Miss Annie for two weeks think? I wondered. And those people from the East Coast, especially the prissy art critic who had talked about Gainesville as though it were the crudest community on Earth?

Later that evening we learned, at least partially, why Miss Annie hadn't been found immediately. There had been no record of her recent purchase of an airline ticket, because she had gotten it months before, when they were running a special rate sale. And she hadn't flown from Gainesville; she'd gotten to St. Louis somehow, and flown to New Mexico from there. Still, Sergeant Leonard said they should have been able to learn all that. He wasn't yet sure how it had happened, he said, but somehow they had missed something.

Chapter Fifteen

DAREN WATCHED MY tape of the news broadcast before we went to the river on Friday morning, and he was amazed by Miss Annie. He had heard that she'd been found, but hadn't seen the actual broadcast.

"At least one big mystery's been solved," he said when it was over. "Now all we have to do is to find Jerred Grayson. Personally, I don't think that's going to happen. He may be mentally unbalanced, but surely he knows that someone will be looking for him after he's made those threats."

I wished I could feel as confident. As nearly as we could tell, the man had learned that it was I who had told the police about the box in the river. He wasn't really dumb, at least, since he'd found out who I was, and that frightened me. Who could ever be sure how such an unstable person as he would behave?

The Lions Club Festival would take place the next day, and I felt bad when I thought about the hundreds of people who would be there, not knowing that the festivities could be interrupted at any moment by Grayson. If only he could be found before the festival started!

On the river, everything progressed almost as on the day before. We saw people in boats and wondered whether they were policemen or just ordinary folks like us. At first a canoe followed us, then we were being followed by two men in a boat. We knew they were water patrolmen. We weren't sure about any of the others, though.

It had indeed been my father and a sheriff's deputy whom I had seen the day before, on the bank. Dad had explained that after letting Daren and me out at Beaver Lodge, he had come to the river at every access to watch us safely pass. So when we came to the same place on Friday, I was comforted to see him there again. I didn't wave or indicate that I even knew him. I felt a bit foolish about it, as though I were acting a part in some silly play. Foolish or not, however, I was glad to see my father at three other access points as we went downstream.

Ever since the boat had replaced the canoe behind us, I had been superficially aware of the sound of the outboard motor. The men would shut the motor off and float, pretending to be fishing until Daren and I had gotten a little distance ahead. Then they would start the motor and come close, sometimes passing us and stopping near the bank to "fish" again until we had once more gotten ahead of them.

From behind us I heard them start the motor to catch up with us, then it stopped running. For the next couple of minutes I could hear the motor start, then falter and die. But soon we had gone too far downstream. We couldn't hear them anymore, and I became increasingly nervous.

"Do you think we should stop and wait for them to get their motor running and catch up?" I asked Daren over my shoulder. There was certainly no way we could paddle the canoe back upstream in that swift current.

"I don't think we ought to stop," Daren said. "We're almost there, and pretty soon another boat or canoe will catch us. We'd better just go on."

"Maybe they had paddles in the boat," I said hopefully. "They might catch us anyway."

"They can't do that," he said. "A boat's harder to paddle than a canoe, and it's a lot slower. But we'll be okay anyway. Surely they have some radios, some kind of communications. They'll send someone soon."

He was right, of course, and I had almost come to agree with him by that time anyway, that Grayson wouldn't show up at all. We weren't very far from Willow Bend by then, and nothing had happened so far.

Still, I drew a sigh of relief when a small boat came upriver toward us, from behind the concealment of an immense willow tree whose branches almost touched the water. The tree leaned at an unbelievable angle. It would topple over into the river in the next windstorm, probably, and it occurred to me that I wouldn't have felt very safe hiding beneath it.

"There's our man now," Daren said. He sounded a bit relieved, too. The boat wasn't a modern one with a jet on it. It had an old propeller motor instead. But the police were using whatever was available, I supposed.

The driver wore a cap pulled low to protect his eyes from the sun, and he wasn't looking at us directly even though he was approaching somewhat nearer than any of the other policemen had done. Perhaps he wasn't one of them after all, I thought, but he didn't have a beard, so he was okay.

Then when he was almost even with us, he did an odd thing. He revved the motor, raising the front end of the boat out of the water, and came directly toward us!

For a second we were frozen, then we reacted together, pulling as hard as we could on our paddles. We shot away from him without more than a foot to spare as the boat skimmed past the back end of our canoe, rocking us from side to side. The canoe came within an inch of scooping up water on one side, then the other.

I was terrified. What was wrong with the man? I wondered. What was he doing on the river if he couldn't handle a boat any better than that? Those propeller blades were viciously dangerous. If he had run over us, we could have been cut to ribbons!

He had turned in a wide circle by then and was again coming toward us. It was insane; was he *trying* to sink us?

Then I saw it—the long, ugly scar on his arm.

"Daren, it's *him*," I screamed just as he revved the motor once more and leaped toward us. I heard the crunching as the side of my canoe caved in, and I saw a glinting piece of metal go sailing through the air, and then I was going under, with my feet tangled or trapped. I swallowed water and fought to straighten myself out. Even in my terror, I wondered that the water around me wasn't red with blood.

At last I released myself when I understood that I wasn't actually trapped. My shoe had hung in the seat brace, and when I slipped my foot out of the shoe, I came to the surface, gasping for air and looking wildly about for the boat. Daren surfaced at almost the same instant, and immediately he came to my side.

The boat was no longer a danger. It had run a little way onto the bank, and though it didn't look to be damaged, we couldn't see Jerred Grayson anywhere.

The canoe floated not far from us, half-submerged and badly damaged. "Let's hang on to the canoe," Daren said, and we swam for it. The water was shallower there, and we could stand and keep the canoe from floating on downstream. Daren kept one arm firmly around me.

I shook so badly, I could barely talk, but I said, "He was trying to kill us, Daren! Where *is* he?"

We turned this way and that, but we couldn't see him. Then we heard the scream of a big jet motor coming upstream.

"Oh God," I said, "don't let it be him!"

But of course, it couldn't have been, and I began to settle down at last when I saw the water patrol insignia on the side of the approaching boat.

In seconds we were safely in the water patrol boat, and two of the three men had swum my canoe to the bank and gone to inspect the boat Grayson had used. I wondered aloud why they weren't trying to find him.

"He can't get very far now," the patrolman said. "Assuming he isn't somewhere under the water, he could only be on that bank, and we already have men on all the access roads. They'll get him."

"I don't see how you can be so sure," Daren muttered. "You didn't keep him from attacking us!"

"We know he didn't put a boat in the river this morning," the patrolman replied. "He must have stolen that one from where someone had it moored. But now he's either drowned or he's on foot. Either way, I think the danger is over now. As soon as we got the call that our men had trouble with their motor a while ago, *everybody* got involved, uniforms and all. If he gets past us, it'll be a miracle."

He directed the two men to remain on the bank in case Grayson returned to the boat, but the men replied that he wouldn't be able to use it if he did return. His propeller had been knocked off when he'd hit our canoe. Without a propeller, the outboard motor was useless.

They remained there, however, and the water patrolman turned and started back downstream.

In just minutes we were at Willow Bend, and we were surprised to see some kind of commotion on the bank there. I leaned forward to get a closer look, and just then Daren yelled, "It's Grayson and Holly's dad!"

They were fighting. How could my father possibly defend himself with one arm in a cast?

Then someone else appeared, and for a moment I couldn't tell who it was. Then I could. It was Sheriff Hooper, and by the time we reached the bank, Jerred Grayson was in handcuffs. He glowered at me. His eyes were positively evil, and I shuddered.

"You're alive!" he growled. "What right you got watching me with those binoculars?"

"You just tried to kill these two kids, didn't you?" my father asked in a terrible, unfamiliar voice. "How dare you complain because they saw you with binoculars!"

"I wouldn't 'a hurt 'em if they'd paid attention to me," he said. "They don't *listen*, that's all. I bashed up their canoe and left her a note so they'd stay away from the river and mind their own business, but they wouldn't pay attention. Rotten kids!"

"You left two notes," Daren said, "and you left out the part about flattening my tires!"

"I didn't do that stuff," the man muttered.

The sheriff and the water patrolman took him away then. I felt a lot better when he was finally out of my sight, but I didn't feel safe until I identified an approaching car as my mother's, and she was holding me tightly in her arms.

Chapter Sixteen

DAREN AND I were elbow-deep in the fiberglass patching materials when Dad said, ''Looks like you've got company, Holly.''

I looked up to see Rhonda Hobbes and Jeannie Smith getting out of Rhonda's car. I had the strangest feeling: it seemed *months* since I had seen my two best girl-friends.

They came into the garage and we greeted one another happily. They had returned from their respective vacations within hours of each other, and had been looking everywhere for me. Being in the middle of repairing the canoe, I couldn't stop, but I talked eagerly. I told them about Grayson, but I didn't tell it in a very organized way, and they grew awfully quiet.

Then I noticed the odd, puzzled look on both their faces, and I couldn't figure out what was wrong until Daren nudged me with his elbow. ''I think it's *me*,'' he said in a whisper loud enough for both of them to hear.

When I understood the confusion, I couldn't resist. ''Gosh, I'm sorry,'' I said. ''I'm just so glad to see you two, I forgot my manners. You do remember Daren, don't you?'' And I casually draped an arm over his shoulder.

''We have been gone *entirely* too long,'' Rhonda said.

"The whole world seems to have changed in the past few weeks."

"Yeah," Jeannie added, "we went off on vacation to get away from dull old Gainesville, and speaking for myself, it was the most boring vacation I ever had. Evidently all the excitement happened *here*."

"Holly, you have a *lot* to tell us," Rhonda said with a nod toward Daren, who was leaning over the canoe then and couldn't see her.

"I guess so," I said, "but not right now. We have to get this canoe fixed in time for the race tomorrow."

"And we've got to pick up our dresses for the beauty pageant before the store closes," Jeannie said, "but as soon as all this is over with . . ."

"Not till after Sunday, girls," Daren said. "Holly and I have a date for Sunday."

"We do?" I asked.

"Yep. We're going to the river and look for eagles."

"Can't," I said. "My binoculars were in the canoe this morning, and they aren't anymore. They're somewhere on the bottom of Spring River."

"Then we'll just *pretend* we're looking for eagles," Daren said.

The canoes were lined up in the water, side by side. There were eleven pairs of us in our mixed-doubles category, six canoes at one boat ramp and five at the other. I sat poised in my front seat while Daren stood in the official starting position on the ramp, ready to push us off and hop in, all in one smooth movement.

On our ramp, there were two gleaming aluminum canoes, one beautiful green one with a painting of an Indian chief on the bow, one in a sky blue that would surely glide as gracefully as a swan—and mine, a sick orange with a thousand scratches and one gargantuan ugly patch visible above the waterline.

The red-haired couple from Riverton were in one of the aluminum canoes, but I didn't actually recognize anyone except one couple, Greg Thomas and Ginger Appleton, in the green canoe. Ginger wore an emerald bikini that perfectly matched the color of the canoe, and her blond curls positively glowed.

I had intended to wear my new swimsuit, until I'd mentioned to Daren that I had bought one especially for the occasion. He had frowned, and said, "As long as it isn't distracting, I guess it'll be all right."

I recalled his earlier remark about Ginger's distracting red bikini, and my heart raced; so seeing me in a swimsuit would really get his attention, would it?

Then he'd said, "Wear it if you really want to, but I think we're going to need every possible advantage. We've been wearing T-shirts and cutoffs all the time, so maybe we ought to stay with the same outfit. Are you sure the new swimsuit won't make you feel less comfortable?"

So much for my ego. There I was in my tacky canoe and my tacky T-shirt and cutoffs. It was the day we had worked so hard for, the day we'd had so much confidence in, and I wasn't nearly as excited about it as I'd expected to be.

The sharp report of the starting pistol split the air then, and all thoughts fled. I dipped my paddle at the precise instant, just as we had practiced, two counts after I felt Daren's weight hit the canoe, and we shot out into the current. We'd been telling one another that we would ignore all the other canoes, but I couldn't help being aware that we had the head start.

We didn't keep it long, for about ten minutes later, I heard someone yell, "Hey, Daren!"

I glanced to the side and saw to my surprise that Greg and Ginger were even with us. I hadn't thought they would be any real competition since they hadn't done much training, but Greg was working hard, and soon they drew ahead.

I didn't actually watch them, but I wondered about their endurance. When I looked up now and then, it was clear that Greg was doing all the work. Ginger was paddling, but I thought they would do even better if she would stop. They weren't working together at all. It was Greg's strength alone that drove them downriver.

We continued at the same pace that we had established during our training, although both of us could have worked harder. It wasn't easy to resist the temptation, but we had promised one another that we would maintain our pace. It wasn't long before the sky blue canoe and the aluminum one paddled by the red-haired couple had both passed us. I clenched my teeth and concentrated on the rhythm, and tried to let the hypnotic effect take over.

There were no boats on the racecourse, only the canoes, but I was vaguely aware that there were people at all the access points. We kept on and on; we didn't wave or respond to their cheers, for we had to devote all our energy to the task at hand. The river was crooked, and we couldn't see very far ahead, but it wasn't long before the three canoes that had passed us were out of sight.

On we went at our determined pace. After what seemed like forever, we could see the sky blue canoe again, and in another thirty minutes or so, we had passed it by. After a while I glanced back, and there wasn't a single canoe in sight behind us.

Another long stretch, and we saw Greg and Ginger, but the red-haired couple were ahead of them. It took a long time for us to pass Greg and Ginger. Greg paddled almost as hard still. Maybe he was strong enough to make it. It looked as though I had underestimated him.

If we could keep our pace, we would at least come in second—but the problem was that the red-haired couple ahead of us were from Riverton! If we didn't overtake them soon, we were going to lose to Riverton after all.

Then we saw the aluminum canoe, and in spite of our vows not to do so, we paddled harder. We were closer than we had thought. We *couldn't* let them beat us!

I focused on the water in front of me, and when Daren said, "Look, Holly, they're in trouble!" I raised my head to see. The aluminum canoe had overturned, and we could see some frantic splashing in the water. Frightened for their safety, we paddled harder than ever to reach them.

The girl was panicked, and the boy wasn't having much luck at helping her. She fought and screamed. And they were in deep water!

When we drew near the couple in the water, Daren said, "Take the canoe, Holly. Stay close. I'm out." He dove so neatly that the canoe hardly rocked at all.

I paddled closer to the nearest bank, ready to dive in myself if it was necessary. But after a moment Daren came swimming strongly, towing the frightened girl. The boy swam more slowly. He was clearly exhausted, but he would make it to the bank.

I saw Greg and Ginger then. They had stopped paddling, and Greg called, "Need any help, Daren?"

Daren yelled back, "We're okay, Greg. Go on and win!"

It seemed a long while before the boy and girl were calmed enough for Daren and me to even consider leaving them, but then we couldn't seem to go. Their canoe had floated quite a distance downstream into a treetop, and we could see the treacherous current jerking it back and forth. Then while we watched, the canoe literally caved in against the limbs, and slowly sank from sight.

After they had thanked us, the boy said, "You two go on now. We'll be all right. You deserve to win. You're good. You can beat the couple in the green canoe."

I looked up to see Daren gazing at me questioningly, but I couldn't say, "Let's go." Neither could he.

Then the girl began to sob. "We tried to stop you," she gasped. "We watched you, and you were so good! We wanted to win, and we . . . tried to scare you off."

"That's right," the boy said, unable to look at us. "We flattened your tires. We even left you a note to scare you. We're so ashamed. We did all that, and now you've saved our lives and lost the race because of it."

For a moment I clenched my teeth in anger, but they were pitiful, and my bad feelings evaporated. I saw Daren watching me then, and there was such tenderness in his eyes! How could I be angry, with that kind of warmth flowing out to me?

Greg and Ginger won the race, of course, and somehow it seemed all right to Daren and me. Later that evening we stood hand in hand watching the beauty pageant, and when the master of ceremonies had announced the final winners of that competition, he thanked everyone for being there.

"And we want everyone to know," he said with a wide smile, "what your participation in today's events has accomplished. The Gainesville and Riverton Lions Clubs met together last night. We decided that the proceeds from this year's festival will be presented to the Livingston Hospital on the East Coast, where David Hooper, our sheriff's son, has just undergone successful surgery to repair the damage to his eyes. Our contribution, made possible by the participation of all of you, will come very close to paying the bill for that surgery!''

The applause drowned out the rest of the man's words, but it didn't matter at all. Daren still held my hand, and he drew me closer to him. I thought for an exciting second that he was about to kiss me right there, and I tingled all over.

Then my parents appeared from nowhere. "The diver went down after the race, and he found the box!" Mom said, her pretty eyes sparkling. "It was tied to a tree root just below the surface, and they were able to pull it up. Grayson made the box at the body shop. It was solidly welded steel and would have lasted underwater for years. You'll never guess what was in it!''

"It was the money from the Cedar Hills bank robbery," Dad said. "Jerred Grayson robbed the bank and hid the money in the Blue Hole. Every cent was there. Sergeant Leonard said he's going to present you two with some kind of commendation for having been instrumental in solving the crime.''

"Instrumental? What does he mean, *instrumental*! We *solved* it!" I said, laughing.

Then in a moment we were alone again in the midst of hundreds of milling people. Daren and I stood facing one another, and I looked up into his eyes.

"Well, we did pretty good, didn't we, Frizz-Head?" he said softly.

"We sure did. We did at that, Jeans," I replied.

About the Author

Nadine Roberts is a teacher of high school English in Naylor, Missouri. She has also written handbooks on taxidermy and stone masonry. Married with three children and six grandchildren, Ms. Roberts nevertheless finds time for boating and camping.